TALES

of the

STORY
KEEPER

RALPH BERWANGER

ISBN 978-1-64670-828-4 (Paperback)
ISBN 978-1-64670-829-1 (Digital)

Copyright © 2020 Ralph Berwanger
All rights reserved
First Edition

All rights reserved. No part of this publication may be reproduced, distributed, or transmitted in any form or by any means, including photocopying, recording, or other electronic or mechanical methods without the prior written permission of the publisher. For permission requests, solicit the publisher via the address below.

Covenant Books, Inc.
11661 Hwy 707
Murrells Inlet, SC 29576
www.covenantbooks.com

This book is dedicated to a boy who hates to read. It is dedicated to a boy who believes that words are his enemy, who wrestles with every word in every sentence. With love, I give this book to that boy. May you find these stories and reading can be your friend.

CONTENTS

Preface 7
Acknowledgments 9
Introduction 11

Papa Rafa, Story Keeper 13
Antonio, My Growing Out of Ordinary 15
Dominic, Driving with the Monkey 27
Giorgio, Becoming a Hat Maker 34
Jeb, My Visit to Washington 42
David, Returning Home 56
Antonio, the Fall of Saigon 66
Terrance, Fighting with the Rebels 72
Antonio, After 9/11 79
Charlie, Camping Alone for the First Time 87
Jeb Daniel, Chasing Wild Boar 99
Jeremy, the Snake 106
Josephine, Talking with Henrietta 112
Silas, the Diving Team 119
Sara, the Ballooning Adventure 129
Francis, Boxing with the Blind 138
Solomon, Face-to-Face with a Lion 148
Pia, Facing the Enemy 157
Isabella, Whale Watching 167
Rafa, My Raft Adventure 178

PREFACE

My first attempt at putting a real book into circulation came at the urging of my children to share stories of my growing up and going out. It was my attempt to let people hear my stories firsthand, not a second- or, even worse, thirdhand telling of what was remembered of the facts as best they could be remembered. I mean, some were from fifty years ago, and we all know what happens to stories that are well-aged. The target audience for that book was my children and grandchildren. If one copy of that book was read by someone outside that group of eleven, publication of the book was a total success. Using that standard, the book was a raving success.

This book is a very different work. It is a book both of historical fiction and pure fiction stories for young people. The stories are purposefully short. Long stories are easily dismissed in favor of a video game or television show. The stories have a point. Each story ends with a challenge for the reader. Actions, decided by the reader, are solicited. Even the story about the talking cat or the monkey and the clown will ask the reader to do something—not change the whole world but maybe a small piece of the one they live in. The stories are meant to be fun. Some stories contain serious topics. They are framed in a way that keeps them from being too heavy. Even a trip through Arlington Cemetery has some lighter moments.

ACKNOWLEDGMENTS

This book was not written in a vacuum. There was help from some great primary sources. The diving story benefited from the firsthand knowledge of divers from the Indiana State swim team. They completely rewrote parts of it based on their own high school diving experience. Young readers and teachers also helped sharpen the author's aim. English students from the Glenwood Middle School in Chatham, Illinois, under the guidance of Jennifer Ferguson, served as a target audience for many of the stories. Their assistance reshaped characters and restructured stories so that they resonate better with young readers. Mary Pyatt Thornton, a history teacher at North Ridge Middle School in North Richland Hills, Texas, and some of Ms. Thornton's students provided valuable encouragement and validation of the book's general design and purpose.

Beyond my thanks to the students and teachers who were my sounding board, there are others without whom this book would not exist. My Puerto Rican brother, Tony Fernandez, was there at the very start of the project. His encouragement after the writing of the first story was the motivation for the next one. He even volunteered to translate the book into Spanish—he was an amazing inspiration from story to story.

My greatest cheerleader was Gena, my wife. As my best friend and champion, Gena, read every word. The high school literature teacher in her helped me find every little error. She used that red pen to lovingly and critically highlight even the most minor problem. Any remaining mistakes remaining in the text are mine and mine alone.

INTRODUCTION

Every story comes from somewhere. Most are not creative works but rather the simple recording of episodes from someone's life. That is where Papa Rafa comes in. Papa Rafa's family has a long tradition of having someone collect and protect stories that belong to their family. He is sort of a family historian. In that role, he not only protects stories from years gone by, he also encourages the current generation to collect and share their stories.

Collected in the pages that follow are just a few of the stories that Papa Rafa maintains. They span multiple generations and are all told in the voice of the real owner of the story.

Why did Papa Rafa choose these stories? Well, there are hundreds of stories in his library. Most of them are simple little tales whose purpose is to capture an important fact about a family member. Some stories are only a couple paragraphs long and might only chronicle a family member attending a reunion. Some are very personal; they would only have meaning to the family. The stories that Papa Rafa includes here are those he thinks will be enjoyed by everyone.

Family Tree

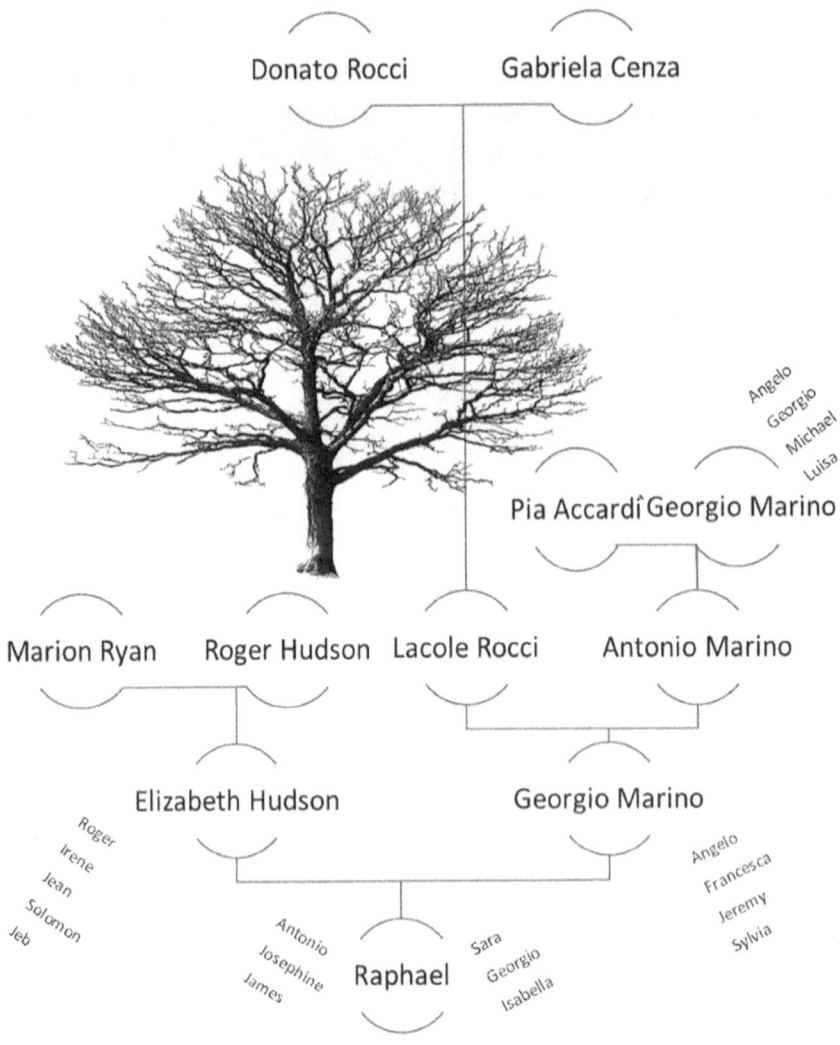

PAPA RAFA, STORY KEEPER

I have been the family's historian for more than forty years. I am searching for someone from the current generation to assume my role, to protect the stories of the past, and to capture new stories from the present. Until I can find my replacement, I will just keep collecting and protecting the stories and history of the family.

I'm Papa Rafa. My real name is Raphael. It is a beautiful name, a powerful name, a name of angels. We had seven children in the family, and I am sure it saved time to just say "Rafa." My father always said, "Be proud of your name. It is who you are." Then, he called me Rafa.

The most important thing about me is that I am the family story keeper. I come from the time of oral tradition, where someone in the family was responsible for knowing and passing on the family's history. Uncle Angelo was before me. He passed away, and the task came to me.

Being the story keeper is demanding. I record when someone comes into the family and when someone leaves. I have stories of births, birthdays, and funerals. I've captured stories told to me by the family about life in the old country and this one. I'm proud to be the story keeper.

When the family gathers, the young ones don't say, "Dance for us, Papa Rafa," or "Sing for us, Papa Rafa." No, they gather around my chair and say, "Tell us a story, Papa Rafa." I paint pictures for them with words. The stories I paint depend on the time of year, the weather, or sometimes just how I felt at the moment. I am only happy when they can see a face from years ago or even smell the garlic on their breath of former family members. Some are convinced that they have met family members who have been gone for over a decade.

Inside the pages that follow are some of those stories. So, come, sit next to my chair while I tell you the stories. Hear the voices of those who were there. Let me help you feel what they felt and learn from them. You see, at the root of every story is a lesson to learn.

Please remember, I am old. I may get unimportant details a little wrong, but the story will be right. I'll do my best to be clear and brief. Sometimes I can go for hours, but few can stay awake that long. I will pick my words carefully. If you listen as carefully, you will see beyond the words to the people and places. I have a habit of inserting myself into the stories from time to time, just to make sure that you can see the pictures in full color. I will do my best to stay quiet and let others tell their stories through me. So now, let's start.

ANTONIO, MY GROWING OUT OF ORDINARY

Antonio is one of my younger brothers. I have many stories of his growing up and leaving home. He and I got into a lot of mischief when we were young. I grew up to write. He grew up a very different person. Antonio spent over twenty years in the air force. He was a senior officer who commanded many. He was a delegate to the United Nations. He even spoke on the floor of the United Nations in Geneva. Antonio led a consulting company until finally retiring to his home where he spends as much time as possible sitting in his little fishing boat. Where Antonio started and how he got to where he is may be found in this story. I will let him tell now. It won't take you very long to figure out that Antonio is the ordinary boy in the story.

* * * * *

Many years ago, there lived an extraordinary, ordinary boy. Up close, he looked just like all the other boys. He stood, head to the ground, the same height as others, give or take a couple of centimeters. Ordinary. He had broad shoulders and strong limbs, but so did other boys who spent time outdoors. Ordinary. His hair was brown with hints of red when the sun hit it just right—most likely from the Irish blood on his mother's side. His eyes were brown. There is no telling who donated those since both parents had brown eyes. Later in life, his eyes turned hazel, but that is not extraordinary. With freckles on his cheeks, mostly straight teeth, and ears that seemed to cup out just a little, he was ordinary.

The boy was at his best when outdoors. His bike and baseball were constant companions. Whether round or pointy, he would spend hours throwing, catching, bouncing, or kicking anything that could be called a ball. Ordinary. When not occupied with playing some game requiring a ball, he rode that bike of his. Not a fancy twenty-one-speed titanium racing bike; no, just a no-name, one-speed, secondhand, red bike. Ordinary.

In his mind, he was an athlete. His favorite feat was to run and leap onto the neighbor's chain-link fence with no hands. He just stood atop the fence, hands on his hips like Superman. Other times, he would march back and forth or run from yard to yard on the top of the fences. Extraordinary. Eventually, he would fall off. Ordinary.

The boy played on the local boys' blub baseball team. Back then, girls were not allowed to join. Now, of course, it is a boys' and girls' club. On the field, he was either playing first base or right field because he was left-handed. Actually, the boy threw a ball with his left hand but wrote his homework assignments with his right hand. That would seem extraordinary, except that he lived in a time when writing with the left hand was discouraged. He was told over and over, "You write with the right." I guess that makes it less extraordinary.

He much preferred football to baseball; maybe that was because the teams were organized by weight, not age. That changed in high school, but before then, things were even. The boy started as a linesman; later he became a running back and linebacker, but during the early days, he was content to block and tackle. Football gave him something that baseball could not. When he dropped a fly ball or swung at an awful pitch, he was standing front and center on stage. There was no hiding his lack of skill or bad judgment. Football was different. A helmet hid his face from everyone on the sidelines when playing football. It was very helpful when he missed a block. There were twenty other boys crowded around him to hide his mistake. He looked like everyone else—ordinary.

The boy liked being hidden in the crowd. He hated being the focus of attention. He rarely raised his hand in class. He might know the answer but didn't want to risk being wrong. Wrong answers were rewarded with giggles from the others and certainly made him feel dumb. A wildly wrong answer caused all-out laughter. Nope, it was better to sit on his hand when he thought he knew the answer than to risk becoming the focus of the class's laughter.

The boy found himself forced to recite portions of poems and read aloud in class far too often. It seemed to be his sixth-grade teacher's favorite torture. The boy hated standing in the spotlight, but what else could he do? He sang in the school's choir for the Christmas PTA meeting, but he was singing with every other child in the sixth grade. Yes, he was a real standout—deep in the back of the group. Ordinary.

Despite all his ordinariness, the boy coasted through elementary school. He made ordinary grades in a system that used grades like "poor," "good," and "very good." The marks were mostly "good," with a few "very good" sprinkled in.

Socially, the boy was part of a clan formed from the boys' club crowd. There were a few outsiders, mostly girls who were barred from being in the boys' club for obvious reasons. The boy was an official member of the clan. He was comfortable with these guys and even took the lead from time to time. He enjoyed the respect that came from his moments of leadership, but he didn't want to lead; he just wanted to belong, in the middle of the third row if possible. Ordinary.

The boy left elementary school and began junior high school. His safe little group was thrown into a pool with dozens of other little groups. If that wasn't enough, adolescence was fast approaching. A whole set of new challenges was about to crash into his life.

At this same time, there lived an extraordinary girl. She lived in the same world as the boy but went unnoticed. Not completely unnoticed, but after all, she was a girl and did not play baseball.

The girl was extraordinary, and well, the boy was not. Her name was Linda. She was the older sister of the boy's friend, Steve. Steve and the boy played on the same baseball team, and Steve was also the son of the baseball coach. It was the baseball team that allowed the extraordinary girl to enter the ordinary boy's world. Linda was the coach's official scorekeeper for every game. She sat on a chair behind the bench and recorded the game's lineup and the result of every batter's time at the plate.

Linda and the boy seldom ever spoke to each other during the first year on the team. To her, he was just another boy under a green baseball cap. Ordinary. That didn't bother the boy because baseball, not girls—especially not an older girl—was his passion.

The second season started just like the first one ended. The boy played baseball and the girl kept score. Gradually, he dared to speak to the girl, mostly when he carried one of the equipment bags back to her father's car. By the middle of the second season, which was during the spring of his sixth-grade year, the boy noticed her more. He did not "like" her, whatever that meant, but he did notice how perfect she wrote the letter K onto the scoresheet after he struck out.

Late spring was warm, and the girl wore shorts to most of the games. This did not escape the boy's notice. She had long legs, which earned her the nickname of "legs" from the boy. She was quick to fling back a nickname for the boy, "tail." It wasn't meant as a compliment, but there was no harm, and thankfully, the name never went beyond the baseball field. An ordinary boy might have a difficult time shedding a label like that, especially in junior high school.

Ah, junior high school. It was there that Linda became truly extraordinary. Junior high school was an entirely different experience from anything the boy had known before. Students wandered from class to class during the day, moving from one end of the building to another. Boys were required to take showers after gym class to protect those who would be in class with them during the rest of the day. It was a giant stall with a hundred showerheads, no shower curtains, just other boys trying to hide from each other. *Ugh.* School lockers, homeroom, the cafeteria, everything needed to be learned. All the things he thought that he knew about school were wrong.

Junior high school took a grand interest in the social life of students. Back then, there was a Friday-night dance at the school almost every month—at least it seemed that way. The tables were rolled out of the cafeteria, and the room was transformed into the junior high version of a dance hall. In true sixties style, local high school bands provided live entertainment. Every band played "House of the Rising Sun" and "Wipeout.". Most copied the Beatles or maybe the Rolling Stones.

Older junior high students were acquainted with the social protocol. They owned the dance floor; in fact, they owned just about everything about the evening. They crowded into the transformed cafeteria to "twist," "watusi," and mingle. Younger students, this would be the boy and his classmates, acted more like castaways marooned on an uncharted island.

Tradition had created specific zones within the dance hall. There were no boundaries drawn on the floor, but they were real, with or without dotted lines. The stage for the band was in the center of the long interior wall. That never changed. To the right of the stage was the entrance to the school's kitchen. The student council refreshment stand was positioned to one side of that door. It consisted of a line of folding tables decorated according to the theme of the night. Regardless of the dance theme, drinks were to the left and baked goods were to the right. The refreshment stand was manned by parents. There might be a teacher or two present. Ms. Papakostas was always there.

Ms. Papakostas was the faculty sponsor to the student council and was always at the tables on dance night. She was a home economics teacher. Who could forget Ms. Papakostas? Memory tells me that she was Greek; that could be wrong. Memory also says that she was young, petite, and perky; that is certain. Ms. Papakostas was a mix of Betty Crocker and Annette Funicello (some may need to look for her on the Internet). The girls flocked around her, giggling about all sorts of things. She was more like a big sister at times than a teacher. The boys wished they could call up the courage to ask her to dance. She was daring enough to say yes, and that was enough to keep them from asking.

Along with working the stand, the adults kept a close eye on the dance floor. Proper dancing required that there always be daylight between the dancing couples—close was okay, too close was forbidden. Where there was no daylight, there was an adult. Oh, do you remember that there were cupcakes? More about that in a minute.

Of course, dancing students filled the center of the room. The older students danced in couples; there were pockets of girls who were dancing with other girls or no one at all. The end of the exterior wall of the cafeteria, the end away from the refreshment tables, was where the seventh-grade girls gathered. They were there with other friends, hoping that someone would ask them to dance. From their zone, the girls could talk, giggle, and point at seventh graders who were brave enough, or silly enough, to go onto the dance floor.

That leaves the seventh-grade boys. The real estate at the other end of that exterior wall—opposite the seventh-grade girls—was the domain of the seventh-grade boys. There is no record of how the boys ended up with this prime location, but they didn't care. Their designated area was next to the cupcake table, and that pretty much defined how the evening was going to go. The boys would lean against the wall, stuffing cupcakes into their mouths while laughing at those on the dance floor. Secretly, every boy wished he were brave enough to ask one of the seventh-grade girls at the other end of the wall to dance, but that was not going to happen. At the end of the night, there might be some cake icing on the tops of their shoes, but it was unlikely that there would be any dust from the dance floor.

To this day, it is not clear why the ordinary boy went to that seventh-grade dance. He owned some fancy footwork, but that was only when he was wearing sixteen-ounce boxing gloves. Those moves were of little use on the dance floor. To dance by himself or with another boy was never going to happen, and there was no chance that he was going to ask a girl to dance. Some of the bravest of his class would not dare that, and he was not among the bravest. So, the boy took his assigned position within the seventh-grade corral and began to eat cupcakes.

Enter the extraordinary girl. The boy did not see her enter. She could have been by herself, with a group of girls, or even with a boy. There were so many crowded into the room that it was hard to know when anyone arrived. It didn't matter if she was there or not. The girl was in ninth grade. By social order, ninth-grade girls didn't talk with seventh-grade boys except to ask them to get out of the way.

Rules were broken that night. Somewhere in the records of the evening, there must be a special note of what happened. It is hard to imagine that it happened today, but it was more unbelievable back then. The boy was standing in his assigned place, being very ordinary. He may have just finished a cupcake; he might have even been brushing the crumbs off his face when it happened.

As unbelievable as it sounds, the extraordinary, ninth-grade girl crossed the cafeteria and walked right up to the boy. Much of the air left the seventh-grade boy's zone as they gasped with terror that a girl, a ninth-grade girl, had entered their area. The girl looked the ordinary boy in the eyes and with a clear, gentle, extraordinary voice asked, "Would you like to dance?"

The band may have stopped playing. The boy was sure that every head in the room turned in his direction. His heart rate doubled, he felt hot all over, and his palms started to sweat. This was a crisis. If he said no, he would be branded as a coward. If he said yes, he would be forced to enter the most dangerous place in the room. If he stumbled or stepped on her foot, his picture would be on the front page of the next day's paper. No matter what happened, the seventh-grade corral would be sure to get a great laugh at his expense.

In the boy's defense, he was familiar with dancing. His aunt Francisca had encouraged, maybe "forced" is a better word, the boy to dance with his cousin many, many times. He owned more skills than he realized thanks to those dance sessions. If he accepted the invitation, he was not unprepared.

With a smile straight from the baseball field, she just quietly said, "Come on, Tail, let's dance." The decision was made. The ordinary boy took her hand and walked into the center of the dance floor. By the time the couple began dancing, the song was near finished. Memories are lost about that song, but the song that followed caught the boy's attention for long after the dance was over. Without notice, the tempo changed, and suddenly the boy was preparing to slow dance with a ninth-grade girl. At first, he thought that the girl would just return to her friends, but their dance was not over. Slowing the tempo didn't change her mind about wanting to dance. She put her hand on his shoulder, and he took her hand. She placed her hand into his, and they just danced. The ordinary boy and the extraordinary girl just danced. There was nothing romantic about the moment, but the boy always remembered the sweetness of the time that they danced.

The song ended; the boy thanked the girl for dancing with him and returned to where his friends were still standing in shock. Cupcake crumbs fell to the floor as their mouths gaped wide. What had just happened? Somehow the dance added height to that boy. He was taller as he moved back among the rest of the boys. Whether or not the extraordinary girl intended it, that dance was a milestone event in the boy's junior high school life. The boy's stock among his classmates went up. Not only had the boy danced, but he danced with a ninth-grade girl. Not only had he danced with a ninth-grade girl, but the girl asked him to dance. At that moment, the boy's greatest victory was not that he danced with the girl, rather that he danced without stepping on her feet and that he did not trip when he returned to the seventh-grade corner. The ordinary boy became a lot less ordinary that night, owing much of the change to an extraordinary girl.

The boy attended many of the dances during that year. He danced at least once each time with the extraordinary girl, not because it gave him status but because the night would not be complete without dancing with "Legs."

Linda's part in the story is much bigger than what is told here. That extraordinary girl was not just a ninth-grade girl; she was an attractive ninth-grade girl. She had a sweet face. Her smile was innocent and kind. If the boy were older, he would have been proud to say that she liked him. But that is not the way it was with Linda and the boy. She was more like an angel that came to the boy's aid and then moved on. She went onto high school, and the boy does not remember ever seeing her again.

The boy's world grew. Linda moved onto high school, and on cue, a new extraordinary girl appeared. This girl was extraordinary in a different sort of way. She may have been as ordinary as the boy, but she caused extraordinary changes in the boy.

It was eighth grade, and just like the year before, a ninth-grade girl popped into the boy's life. Now the boy was less ordinary than in past years, but honestly, he was far from extraordinary.

The boy's algebra class had both eighth- and ninth-grade students. There were a few ninth-grade students who sat in the last few desks on the far-right side of the room. The boy sat in the last eighth-grade seat in front of the ninth-grade students. A girl named Gomer sat directly behind the boy—that is something that you just don't forget. Behind Gomer sat Sandy. Sandy was extraordinary girl number two.

This extraordinary girl captured the boy's attention immediately. She was a Scandinavian blonde with bright blue eyes. She wore braces, but they were very attractive braces. Her eyes twinkled, and her smile caused the boy's head to turn toward the back of the row more than once.

The girl and boy started the year with only one common point of interest—algebra. The boy had always had a gift for math. As ordinary as the boy was, math topics always came easy to him. Numbers were better friends than words sometimes. While early lessons focused on basic principles of numbers, the basic number that the boy was seeking was the girl's phone number. As he looked back, that may have been one of the boldest things the boy had done up to that point in his life. Of course, the reason for exchanging phone numbers was to share homework and to talk through problems from the day's class. Conversations went all over the place, but they started and ended with homework.

By the middle of that year, the boy developed a full-grown crush on the girl. In the whole of human history, there has never been a more one-sided relationship. The boy was gaga, and the girl was oblivious. She was not mean, just completely unaware.

The boy wasn't crazy. There was no way that he could let her know how he felt. She was everything that he was not; she was a ninth grader. It was easier just to admire her from a distance. He would race from wherever he might be in the school to be at the bottom of the stairs as she was going to class—it appeared that they just ran into each other. He went over to her house a few times and even rode in the car with her after she got her driver's license.

It doesn't seem possible, but the boy never told her about how he felt—never. He spoke with her from time to time during his ninth-grade year, but she was in high school, so they didn't see each other. They were in the same school again starting in his sophomore year. Like in earlier days, he would meet her on the way to lunch and share a brief conversation. It was easier in high school since they ate at the same time.

The final meeting of these two was abrupt. It was late in the fall. The boy was leaving school, moving to Florida, and would never see her again. His parents agreed to delay the move until Thanksgiving; this way, he could play in the homecoming football game. Just for the record, delaying the move had nothing to do with the girl; the boy was a starter on the junior varsity team and wanted to play in that game.

The JV played its game the day before the varsity homecoming game, on Thursday. So, on Friday morning, the boy went into school for the last time. Books were returned, and the withdrawal process was completed by lunch. He planned that his last act would be to go to the lunchroom and tell the girl good-bye.

He was approaching the cafeteria when the girl met him; she was bubbly with the excitement of homecoming week. She took his hand and told him that she had seen him return the kickoff at the start of yesterday's game. It was a remarkable run. With the finesse of a ballerina, the boy dodged and twisted his way down the field, starting at the ten-yard line. He didn't score. He met a wall of players from the other team in a thundering crash, so his advance stopped twenty-five yards short of the goal. Still, it was an impressive run, and the girl did see it. That made it as good as scoring. His team lost that game in the final minutes, but at that moment in front of the cafeteria, who remembered that?

The boy stopped the girl to report that he was leaving, that he would not be back. He had planned to tell her that he had always liked her. This was not a Romeo and Juliet sort of thing, but he did want to tell her that he had liked her for a long time. He wanted to tell her that she was special and that he was going to miss her. A speech had been rehearsed in his head, but not one word of it came to mind. At that moment, he just shook her hand, said good-bye, and walked away. Regret always returned to him when he recalled that short space of time.

This story did not end until the boy started school in Florida. He had no idea if that extraordinary girl missed him or ever thought anything more about him. He was sure that in his ordinary way, he acted cowardly. Playing it over and over in his mind, he asked himself, "What did I have to lose by telling her how I felt?" After all, he was leaving. Wrestling with that moment began the process of turning the Mr. Ordinary into someone, well, a little less ordinary.

"What do I have to lose?" That question was haunting. It became the question that he asked over and over as he met people and new challenges. More often than before he took risks, often it was not as bad as he feared. That same boy that hid within the cast of the sixth grade Christmas pageant, trying to be as invisible as possible, played Banquo in the high school production of *Macbeth*. He was the most convincing ghost that ever stepped onto the stage. Frightened? Yes. The best Shakespearian actor in the school? No. Still, there he was, pushing through fear. The legacy of the departure from that extraordinary girl deserves credit for this change.

There you have it, the story of a boy and two extraordinary girls. But there is more to the story. Over the years, the boy dated and danced with many girls—one he married. Why aren't some of those girls included? Where was the story of Patty, the girl he took to the senior prom? Why didn't he include a story about meeting Gena and their marriage? What makes these two very old, silly stories so important? Well, there is more to the story.

The boy had a chance to talk with Linda and Sandy years after the events of this story were over. Both women, now older with families of their own, had the same response to the story. Sandy did not only not know that he had a schoolboy crush on her, but she didn't remember him at all. Those were her exact words, "I'm really sorry, but I don't remember you at all." The words were a little different, but Linda's response was very close to the same.

Neither girl remembered who he was. Each had a profound impact on him, at different times in his life, and neither knew it. There hides the importance of this story.

It must make us stop and think. We move and live in a community. There are people we watch, who encourage us, who help us. It would be nice if they knew about it now, not twenty years from now. Also, people are watching us, people whom we will help and encourage. Some meek people will become brave. Some quiet people will find their voice. Talent hidden inside of a friend will be exposed and nourished because of us. All of this without our knowledge.

One last little thing. You should know that every word of this story is true. I know it is because I was that boy. I know me better than anyone else and can tell you that I was at my best when I was being ordinary. What's more, that is all I ever wanted to be. These two girls helped change all of that.

* * * * *

Out the Book and Into the Street

We cannot always know those whom we affect. It is wise to remember that people are watching us, that what we do, how we treat them, can be with them for a lifetime. For that group, we just hope that our impact on them is for their good. What about the others? What about the "I never knew" folks? Could you let them know that you are standing a little taller because of them? Out on the street with you, go find them before forty years have passed.

DOMINIC, DRIVING WITH THE MONKEY

My nephew Dominic can entertain the family for hours with his stories. Dominic is the middle son of my sister Sylvia. He grew up in New York City and has driven a taxicab in that city for years. He has stories of famous sports players and rich business executives who were his passengers. Most stories are just about the ride and how the riders treated him. Most of these stories, I forget shortly after their telling; there are just too many stories for me to keep them all. Most of the stories that I kept about Dominic are about his growing up. Still, there are some stories about his taxi adventures that will always remain with the family story keeper. This is my favorite story about Dominic's taxi driving. See if you agree that it is as fun as I do.

*****

I've been driving a cab in Manhattan for almost twenty years. In that amount of time, you see a lot of things. Honestly, some things you just would not believe. Rich, poor, locals, tourists, I see them all. There is one trip that I won't ever forget.

It was just after Thanksgiving, three years back. It was turning cold, but not like late January when the wind cuts right into your bones. The Thanksgiving parade was over; most of the folks who came to town for the parade were gone. Christmas lights were up everywhere, and the bell ringers were on every other corner. The Christmas season in New York is a great time for taxi drivers, especially in Manhattan. There are lots of short trips—short trips mean smaller fares but better tips.

It was late evening, about eight o'clock, when I picked up a fare on 76th Street over by the Hudson River. Like I said, weather this time of year can be nasty. It was above freezing. There was rain, mixed with snow, being pushed across the city by a rather stiff breeze. No one wanted to be out in that stuff.

I arrived at a hotel to find that my fare was a middle-aged woman. She was well dressed, her appearance suggested that she was well off—there could be a good tip in this ride. In her arms, she was holding a small monkey.

Now I must tell you, people in New York like their animals. I am always taking some dog owner and his canine friend somewhere in the city. More than once, I have been the animal ambulance for an ailing mutt. I have had birds, cats, and even snakes in the backseat of the cab. I have strict rules about pets in my cab. After all, they shed, and sometimes they do worse. I don't have time to clean out the cab after every trip, so I have rules. Rule 1 is, "The window of the cab on the pet's side must always be down." There are no exceptions. The animals need air, and I don't need to clean up the cab.

So, when the lady wanted to put her monkey in my cab, I announced rule 1. She complained that it was cold and raining, so I agreed to have the window halfway down. If the window didn't go down, the monkey wasn't going to go in; there was no negotiating.

The lady and her monkey got into the backseat, the window rolled down, and she announced that she needed to go to an address on the north side of Central Park. She said she was going to a party at a friend's condominium. I have been to a lot of parties, and I can't remember one where the guest list included a monkey. I was told that the monkey's name was Finley, and that he was very friendly. Unless Finley was paying the fare for the ride, I didn't care.

The weather made a mess of traffic on the island, and I had to go around the south side of Central Park instead of the way I would normally take. The ride was going to be longer, but the cost of the ride would be better for me—it would make up for the monkey in the backseat.

Traffic was moving but moving slowly. The monkey was staring out the window at the Christmas lights and somewhat mystified by the sleet that was striking the side of the cab. I turned down 70th Street and was just passing the School of the Blessed Sacrament when I spotted Father Efraim standing on the sidewalk under a big black umbrella.

Father Efraim is the best. I have been a member of his parish since forever. He may know me better than my mom. There was no way I was going to let my favorite priest stand out in this weather, so I pulled up and asked him to get in. I've given him a ride many times. Most times, I let him sit up front with me; I don't ever start the meter.

He popped into the front seat without a word. It was easy to see that he was cold and needed a warm place to sit. I offered him some coffee from my thermos, which he accepted with a smile. He hugged the cup between his hands and held his face over the cup letting the steam flow over his face. He really is a very special priest. I knew that Father Efraim was not going in the same direction as the lady with the monkey, so I promised to take him home after we got the lady to her party.

My priest struck up a conversation with the lady, intrigued by her little friend. He wasn't silly enough to try to talk to the monkey, but he did have questions about the lady's unique pet. She told him that like me, she was Catholic, the monkey was not. Their conversation went on without any input from me. The weather was getting worse, and I needed to watch the road.

We made it as far as 57th Street, almost in front of Carnegie Hall, when I saw him. Standing on the corner was a rather large man, dressed as a clown, smoking a cigar. He was getting pelted by the sleet. He didn't have a coat, and there was no umbrella. He was just standing there waiting on someone, a clown smoking a cigar.

I sat waiting for the traffic light to change and began to feel sorry for this clown. Maybe it was the priest in the front seat that was making me feel guilty; regardless, I just couldn't let him stand out in this weather. Father Efraim rolled down his window and asked the clown if he wanted a ride. He hesitated at first, investigated the sky, and then made his way to the cab. Seeing that a passenger was sitting behind Father Efraim, he made his way around to the other side of the cab and started to get in. I told him there was no smoking in the cab, especially cigars. If he wanted to ride, he had to lose the cigar before getting in. Sleet slapping him in the face helped him do the right thing and get into the cab.

The clown crawled into the backseat. He was in terrible shape. The clown suit that he was wearing was soaked, and the rain had turned his clown face to a blur of colors. He tried to wipe some of the water off his face, and that just made things worse. It turned out that the clown was trying to make his way uptown. It was a couple miles past where the lady and the monkey were going, but in that weather, well it would be my good deed for the day. The clown said that everyone called him Rusty then settled back for a warm ride. It was good to get his name because it would have been awkward to keep saying "Mr. Clown."

Father Efraim is a real outgoing guy. He can talk to a phone booth. Before we arrived at the next red light, he had struck up a conversation with Rusty. I really wasn't paying much attention; the roads were slick, and people were crossing here and there to get out of the weather.

Up to that point, Finley had taken no notice of Rusty—he was too busy with the lights and sleet. All that changed in a moment. Maybe it was the new voice in the cab, maybe it was the smell of the cigar smoke that lingered on Rusty. Whatever it was, Finley looked straight into the face of the clown and went crazy. I have heard that a lot of people are afraid of clowns. I can tell you firsthand that there is at least one monkey that doesn't like them.

The monkey leaped into the lady's lap and tried to climb inside her coat. She tried to comfort him, but it didn't help. He would look at the clown and begin his craziness all over. Poor Rusty didn't know what to do. He moved as far away as he could, but it was a taxicab, and the three of them were in the backseat.

Things were getting worse. Father Efraim was trying to help, but this was way outside his normal priestly duties. The woman tried to distract Finley, but each time Finley looked across the seat, the clown was still there. We were on 5th Avenue, up near 72nd Street, when Finley had all that he was going to take from the clown. He wiggled and fought with the woman until he was free and then shot out the open window. Gone!

The woman let out an ear-piercing squeal, which caused me to slam on the brakes. I thought maybe the monkey had bitten her. Rusty and the priest sat there in shock having seen the monkey bolt out the open window. Both doors on the right side flew open, and in flash, Father Efraim and the woman were after the monkey. I moved the car to the curb and followed them. The monkey ran into Central Park with the three of us in hot pursuit.

The weather was getting worse. The rain was now mixed with snow, and it was beginning to fall much faster. It was dark and cold, and I was in no mood to be hunting a monkey in Central Park. For all I cared, Finley could climb a tree and spend the night. I was losing time, losing money, and there was a clown still sitting in the back of my cab.

We wandered through the park for fifteen or twenty minutes. We would catch a glimpse of Finley as he ran from one bush to another, down a path, or up a tree. The lady called to Finley, but he was having no part of anything that might include a clown.

We chased Finley for a few more minutes and found him sitting atop a large mushroom surrounded by the White Rabbit, the Mad Hatter, and Alice. I cannot tell you how odd this whole picture looked. Finley was seated on top of the Alice in Wonderland statue. Any other time, it would have made me laugh, but at that moment, I had no "funny" left in me. I was freezing. I just wanted to grab that monkey and get back to my cab.

Just then, a park policeman rode up on his horse. He had seen the abandoned cab and was checking that everything was all right. The man on horseback made the scene complete. I explained as best I could what had happened. There was no way to report what was going on without it sounding like I was making it up. The policeman was laughing so hard by the time I got to the part about the clown and Finley jumping out the window that I just stopped explaining.

Finley had finally calmed down when Rusty showed up. Rusty felt bad that he had caused such a ruckus and wanted to help. Sadly, that was not what happened. Finley caught sight of the clown, now shrouded in the lights from the park and snow all around. If you can believe it, he looked worse than when he was in the cab. The monkey howled a cry that could be heard all over the park and shot off in the direction of the cab. The policeman took off after him. It was a strange procession made worse by the weather. The monkey fled, chased by a man on horseback, a clown now transformed into something ghoulish by the rain, a priest, a woman wrapped in a soggy fur coat who appeared more animal than human, and me. It had to be the worst night of the monkey's life.

Finley didn't go too far. He sprinted a couple hundred yards and popped up into a tree, maybe twenty feet off the ground. The park police almost caught up with Finley before he sprang into the tree. The rest of our cold, wet group arrived a minute or so later. The lady pleaded with Finley, but he was not coming down.

Rusty, not so much a clown now thanks to the rain, arrived last. The rain, sleet, and snow had washed most of the paint off Rusty's face. What had not been washed off had been wiped off as Rusty ran to catch up with the group. He was still wearing a clown suit, but it was clear that there was a man inside the suit.

"Why Russell Harrigan! Why didn't you tell me it was you?" It turned out that Rusty the clown was also Mr. Russell Harrigan. Father Efraim was obviously as surprised as Finley. Father Efraim knew Russell from the neighborhood. More than once, Father Efraim had eaten at the lunch counter of the local diner with Russell. He just couldn't believe that he had been talking with Rusty all that time and did not see that Russell was underneath the face paint.

Priests have a way of bringing the confession out of a person. Right away, Russell volunteered, "Well, I guess that I didn't want you to see me this way. I mean, I'm a clown and all."

I had to look at him a long time before I realized that I too had seen him before. It's funny. With the paint on his face, I would have never known it was him.

Russell called up to the monkey and coaxed him down. The park police backed away, and the lady continued to call to Finley. It took a few minutes, but Finley eventually decided that Russell was not as frightening as he first appeared. He was cautious as he came down, but before much longer, Finley was back in the lady's arms. At that point, we made short work of getting back to the cab.

I turned the heat all the way up and ordered that the window in the back be rolled up. No one argued. I wanted everyone to be warm, and I didn't want that monkey trying to get out of the cab again. There was a lot of laughter in the cab after we started warming up. The lady decided to skip the party and go home, so we took Russell home first. Finley even gave Rusty a monkey kiss before leaving the cab. The lady was next to be let out. I was going to need some time to talk to my priest after that ride was over.

* * * * *

Out the Book and Into the Streets

Some people like clowns, others are terrified, but behind every clown face is a real person. You might be surprised to know that lots of people put on a face to hide just like Russell became Rusty. They don't think that people really like the "Russell," so they become "Rusty." Today's challenge is to help a Rusty. Let someone know that you like them just the way they are. Tell them something that makes them special without having to put on paint and a big red nose.

GIORGIO, BECOMING A HAT MAKER

It is a good time to look back further into the family. This is a story from my uncle Giorgio. He is my great-uncle, but no one ever called him Great-Uncle Giorgio. This is sort of difficult to explain, so pay attention. I, Papa Rafa, am Raphael, the son of Giorgio. My father, Giorgio, is the son of Antonio, who was my grandfather. My grandfather's younger brother was also Giorgio. In fact, my uncle Giorgio claimed more than once that my father was named after him. That was not actually the case. Uncle Giorgio's father was also named Giorgio. My father was named for Giorgio, my great-grandfather, and not Giorgio the great-uncle. Like a lot of old families, some names repeat from generation to generation; maybe that will help you understand the twisted branches of my family tree.

My uncle Giorgio left Italy as a young man and moved to London, England, where he spent the last eighty years of his life. He was there long enough to lose most of his Italian accent and develop an almost-native Cockney accent. So, now that we understand who Uncle Giorgio is, let us have him tell you the story of his hat.

* * * * *

I am Giorgio Donato Marino. I was born in Padova, Italy, in 1905. I stayed there until a couple of years after the end of the Great War. Like most wars, that war was misnamed. As I remember the war years in our small town in northern Italy, I can think of nothing great about it.

I left Padova soon after the war ended determined to see the world. I traveled across France, walking and catching rides on trucks or trains when I could, and got as far as London. I've made many trips to other parts of the world since then, but I always return to London.

I was nineteen years old when I arrived in London. I spoke broken English with a strong Italian accent. I had very few skills and even less money. What I did have was a willingness to work hard. I took any job that paid real money. I'm sure that I couldn't have made it across France if I'd been picky about the kind of work that was available.

I searched the streets of London for any job. Several very dirty jobs kept me fed for the first few months. The work was hard, the days were long, the pay was bad, but I ate and had a dry place to sleep.

One late spring evening, I was walking in Chelsea when I wandered upon a small hat shop. I would later learn to call it by its proper name. The sign over the front door read *Devon Millinery Shoppe*. A small sign in the window contained a very short message, "Wanted—Milliner Apprentice." I didn't know what a milliner was or what an apprentice did but working in the little shop had to be easier than unloading coal from barges on the Thames River using a shovel.

It was in that shop that I first I met Master Oliver Devon. He was the owner and the master milliner. I called him Master Devon until the day that he died. Anyway, Master Devon was well into his senior years. You'd never detect his real age without a lot of study. He was a tall slender man with a slight bend as he stood. His eyes were bright, his voice was clear, and his hands were weathered. He was black from his fingertips to the second knuckle on both hands from the dye that he used to color his hats. He knew right away from my appearance that I was not there to purchase a hat. In the most direct and somewhat abrupt voice, he asked, "Are you here to apply as my apprentice?"

I shook my head to show interest, which broke loose a chain of questions. Who was I? Where was I from? What had I done? I could hardly finish answering one question when another was flung at me.

Finally, Master Devon changed the interview and began to explain the apprentice position.

Master Devon expected me to be in the shop six days every week. Sundays the shop would close, and he expected that I would take care of personal responsibilities on that day. Workdays would start early each morning and would not end until after dark on most days. Master Devon said that I would do whatever he asked me to do when I was asked. From his description, it sounded like my coal-shoveling job might be easier.

Master Devon had some good news for me. I was not going to get paid very much. It would not be enough to rent an apartment or regularly buy food. At that point, I was not convinced that I wanted to be an apprentice. Master Devon explained that he and his wife lived in an apartment over the shop. There was a small room in the back of the shop where I would be allowed to stay—no need to pay rent. Master Devon also said that I would eat my meals in his apartment. Their food was simple but would be filling—no need to buy food. Finally, Master Devon explained that I would be learning to be a milliner. Over time I would become "a man who knew the fine art of hat making." Someday I might even be Master Marino. This offer was a lot better than shoveling coal. We agreed that I would start the first thing the next day. I would have breakfast with the Devon family and spend my first night in the backroom of the shop.

Master Devon was a teacher. Sometimes lessons were just rules. Sometimes there were demonstrations. As time went on, I performed every task of hat making. The lessons started with simple things and got more difficult over time. His first rule as I was never to call his little art studio a hat shop. There are hat shops all over London but only a very few millinery shops. Saying "hat shop" would earn me a slap on the back of the head or extra nasty jobs at the end of the day. I was an employee of a millinery store, really a fancy name for a hat store but a hat store where hats were made by skilled hat makers. These were not mass-produced on some assembly line; each hat was carefully made by hand. "Millinery," I don't think I'd ever heard that word before I met Master Devon.

Rules two and three were delivered the first week that I worked for Master Devon. They were repeated a thousand times over the years. Rule two: Put a label with your name in every hat that you make. Rule three was simply, "Remember that your name is in every hat." These rules were meant to demand the best out of every hat that was made in the shop and to remind me that protecting my name was important. All the rules that followed were built upon those two.

I spent fifteen years as Master Devon's apprentice. By the end of my apprenticeship, I was able to make hats that matched the work of my master. The other thing that happened over those fifteen years was that the Devons became as close to me as my parents. Eat at someone's table for fifteen years, and you will see how devoted you become to that person.

Master Devon retired the year I completed my apprenticeship. The master agreed to pass on his shop and legacy to me when he finally quit making hats. I purchased the millinery and agreed to never change the name. To this day, the sign over the door reads *Devon Millinery Shoppe*.

Master Devon and his wife moved into a small cottage outside of London, and I moved into the apartment that they occupied for decades. I later married and moved my wife into that apartment where we still live today.

Hat making became my passion. I made hats for women, but my real love was making men's hats. Make no mistake, I've made some very bold lady's hats for very well-to-do women. No matter how beautiful the hat was, it seemed to disappoint me. I remember one felt and silk hat. It had a very wide, floppy brim. The hat was dyed a bright blue with a matching silk band around the crown of the hat. The customer provided me with a large peacock feather that she wanted to be attached to the crown so that it draped over the back of the hat. The hat was breathtaking, and most people would pay richly to own a hat like that—the lady who bought it did just that. My problem is the hat hides the woman under it. I am sure that my father is the reason I feel this way. I remember when I was a boy. We would be finishing dinner. My papa would place his rough hands under my mama's chin and say, "Boys, look at what God has done.

Have you seen anything more beautiful than this today?" Mama would smile, sometimes let out a little giggle, and then swat him with a dish towel and tell him to behave himself in front of us boys. From my papa, I just knew that these women were made by a craftsman with far greater skill than me, and it seemed a shame to hide them under my hats.

That is exactly why I prefer making men's hats. My hats protect hair from the wind. My hats protect heads without hair from the sun. The hats are tasteful but don't distract from the wonder of the one below them. I make a variety of men's hats: top hats, bowlers, fedoras, and trilbies. Top hats have been worn for years. The American president, Abraham Lincoln, is often pictured wearing a stove-top, top hat. Fedoras and trilbies are the most popular hats now. These hats can be worn by rich and poor. They are functional and look good with a handsome suit or open-collar shirt. I even made a pork pie hat for a chap from America. It was a gray hat with brown silk trim. It was too silly for Londoners, but it seemed to fit him. To be honest, I would rather make bowler hats. Bowlers, derbies, or bombin, call them what you want, these hats have the most character.

When hat making is done right, it is a slow process. I repeat the steps that Master Devon taught me for each hat. No step is skipped, and each is skillfully completed before moving to the next. Still, sometimes something is missing when I finish the last step. It isn't a missed step; it is just something about the hat that does not seem right. That brings me to *the* hat.

It was late in the winter of 1944. The next great war had been going on for many months, and London was under constant attack. Too many nights the sirens would sound, and we would take shelter in the underground while bombs were going off over our heads. Many parts of London were just rubble, and there were damaged buildings all over Chelsea. Somehow, Devon's Millinery Shoppe was spared. We had windows that were cracked or broken, but the building stood just as it had all the years that Master Devon owned it. Even the sign over the door was unscratched.

I tried to work in my shop every day, just as I did before the bombing began. Sometimes I could not find material for new hats.

In those times, I was creative using whatever I could find. Sometimes I would take apart hats that seemed to need some attention and remake them. I stayed busy.

On the winter day that I mentioned, I set out to make one of my standard bowler hats. I used the best felt to make the bowler. I seem to remember that it was the last of the material that I had. I followed each step just as I had a hundred times before. I brushed the felt and steamed the brim. When it was done, I put the hat onto a stand and placed it on the shelf with a few other bowlers that were awaiting new owners.

I was never fully happy with that hat. I believed something was not right with the hat but didn't know what. I took it apart twice to resew the brim onto the crown. It was no use. The hat was lesser than the other bowlers that were waiting on the shelf. I went so far as to remove the label from inside the hat. I put it back in later, but I can tell you that the poor hat sat on the shelf for several days with no label—a clear violation of rule two.

In late January of the next year, a gentleman came into the shop looking for a hat. He said that his employer needed a new derby. The employer was too busy to come himself, so this gentleman had come to pick out a hat. Normally it helps to have the head of the man who is going to wear a hat. That's the best way to get a good fit. The gentleman said that his employer would not come. He had brought one of his employer's old hats that I could use to fit the size. It was a very worn bowler that stank of stale cigar smoke. As goes hats, the gentleman's employer had a large head, but I had a couple that would fit the fellow.

The gentleman was directed toward two shelves of bowlers that could be made ready. I was surprised when the gentleman picked out the hat that I had taken apart multiple times, the one that I was sure had something wrong with it. I attempted to redirect the gentleman to other hats on the shelf, but he was certain that this was the right one for his employer.

There was no changing his mind. Since I couldn't interest the gentleman in a different hat, I promised to ready the hat before the end of the week. The hat would have to be stretched, pressed, and neatly packed into an appropriate hat box before it would leave the store. I considered removing the label from the hat, but that made no sense. The gentleman knew where it had come from. If the hat pleased his employer, others would come to my millinery. If the employer saw the same invisible flaw in the hat that had distracted me for weeks, well, I would probably never have his business again.

The gentleman arrived exactly as promised, paid for the bowler, and took it away.

Now there is one thing that I have not said. Every milliner knows his hats. Put a milliner's hat with a dozen others, and the milliner will pick out his hat every time. It could be the shape of the brim or the way that the crease is pressed into the top of the hat's crown. It is not easy to explain how the milliner knows his hat, but he knows his hat.

That brings me to the final part of this hat's story. I was having breakfast and reading the *London Times* in late February of 1945. The next great war was about to be over, and the paper was full of news about meetings between the US president and the British prime minister. There on the front page of the paper was a picture of Prime Minister Churchill sitting beside President Roosevelt. There on Mr. Churchill's lap sat a very neat bowler. I could not have been any surer of that hat's beginning if the *London Times* had printed a picture of the label from inside the hat. It was my hat. The gentleman chose that hat to sit atop one of the most important men in the world—a hat that I always felt was missing something. Mr. Churchill's gentleman was able to see the quality of the hat while I was too busy trying to improve it.

I've made hats for many important people, even British royalty, but no hat has ever been more special to me than that old bowler that I didn't think was worthy of wearing my label. Hopefully, you won't be surprised to know that the gentleman who bought that hat in the winter of 1945 visited the Devon Millinery Shoppe several times in the years following the war—each time to purchase a new bowler for his employer.

* * * * *

TALES OF THE STORY KEEPER

Out the Book and Into the Street

Sometimes we just don't see what is clear to others. Uncle Giorgio saw flaws where perhaps none existed. At the very least, he considered it less valuable than others. That hat sat on top of Mr. Winston Churchill. Maybe, it's not a hat that you don't think is perfect enough. It could be a project you are working on, a drawing, or a model. It could be someone that you know, a neighbor. In either case, today would be a good day to step back and try to see what others see and enjoy the true worth of that person or thing.

JEB, MY VISIT TO WASHINGTON

I could tell stories all day about my uncle Jeb. All his friends called him Biscuit. There are lots of stories about how he got that name, but we'll have to wait for a later time to talk about that. Jeb doesn't sound very Italian, it's not. My mother was born in the Smokey Mountains. Her family farmed a small piece of land that was able to put food on the table for their family of eight. My mother was the oldest of the eight, then there were twin girls, Irene and Jean Ann, Uncle Jeb, Uncle Solomon, and Uncle Nathan. Uncle Nathan was the baby. There are not many stories about Uncle Solomon; he died in Vietnam in '62.

So, here is a story that I recently got from Uncle Jeb. It is not so much about him as it is about what he thought was important. I am sure that he would hope it was important to you too.

* * * * *

Late spring mornings in Washington, DC, are beautiful. The morning air is crisp; the skies are bright and clear, and the cherry blossoms are in full bloom. Children are on break from school, so the city is brimming with visitors. Long lines to get into the museums grow longer as the morning goes on. Seats on the city tour buses are seldom vacant. You are wise to buy a spot on the tour days in advance. That is exactly what I did.

I bought Bethany and me tickets on one of the city tour buses. I could have walked, but Bethany gets tired after a couple hours. I found this small tour called America the Great Tour Company. Just the name alone was enough to get my money. Later I find out that the company is owned by this fellow named Luka and that he only had one small bus. He opened the company a couple years earlier after spending five years as a tour guide for a larger company in town. The company that Luka was with was preparing to retire one of its small commuter buses, so Luka bought it and *"America the Great"* Tour Company was born. Now this guy spends six days a week, ten hours a day, presenting tourists with facts and trivia about the history of the nation's capital. I began to wonder if I made the right decision when the bus pulled up to the pick-up point that morning.

Friday mornings are normally not very busy, that's because Washington visitors normally return home on Friday. It was 12:45, and this Friday was normal. Luka's earlier tours were not full, and only twelve people are signed up for ours. The bus seated twenty paying customers, and empty seats represent lost money. I suppose he could have looked at it by saying that twelve riders were better than nothing. Still, we found out that Luka had four kids at home. I could have squeezed two more customers into the front seats if it were me, but Luka reserved those seats for a cooler with his lunch and bottled water for his guests. Only the best for guests of *America the Great Tours.*

Luka started inviting us onto the bus right on time. The air-conditioning and upholstered seats were more inviting than the steel park bench where Bethany and I had been sitting, so there was no argument from me.

Each member of the group was warmly greeted with a strong handshake and Luka's introduction. "Hello, good to see you. I am Luka and will be your driver and guide today. And what are you called?"

The first to board the bus was the Bower family from Wisconsin. The husband introduced each member of his clan. It was difficult to forget them since every name started with the letter R—Randy, Rachael, Robin, and Ryan. Ryan was called RB by the family. He was the youngest, so I suppose that he could have been called "RD" or "R4," but their last name was Bower, so "RB" made sense too. The husband and wife were without jackets and in short sleeves. The children were dressed in shorts. The girl was wearing what looked like a new T-shirt with a picture of the White House. The boy's T-shirt was bright red with "Badgers" written across the front.

Next were two retired couples from Florida: Jeff, Trish, Steve, and Peggy. These folks were just starting their time in Washington. Jeff and Trish looked too young to be retired. Jeff was a little short of average. Judging from his polo shirt, shorts, and tan, Jeff spent a lot of time playing tennis back home. There was no mistaking Trish's passion. Clearly printed on the front of her sweatshirt was a picture of two small children with the caption, "Nana's Angels." Steve also sported a dark tan. That is where the similarities with Jeff ended. Jeff kept his gray hair cut close to the scalp. Steve had lost all the hair from the top of his head. Also, Steve stood at least one head, maybe two heads, taller. Steve might be a tennis player, but it was more likely he was drawn to basketball. Steve's wife, Peggy, was years younger than he. She was bubbly, quick to announce that she had never been to Washington before and anxious to get started.

We were the next group to board the bus. I told Luka that all my friends called me Biscuit, and he could do the same. I had my ball cap announcing pride in my service during Vietnam and that tattered and faded old green vest that I wear from time to time. Bethany had resewn a couple of the patches from my old units to make it more presentable. You should see that old vest. Some of my buddies have written on the back of the vest in black marker. Some of those guys are gone now. As always, Bethany was dressed for touring. She had on those pink walking shoes that she takes everywhere. I guess we could have walked instead of taking the tour after all.

Two teenagers were the last to board the bus. The boy mumbled something when asked his name; I don't think that Luka ever knew what he said—I don't think anyone did. The girl was cheery; she giggled a lot. She said her name was Vivian and that she would really like to be called Biscuit. I told her that name was already taken and that there were probably better names for her to pick.

The teenagers were either local high school kids or college kids from the look of it. I can't tell the difference anymore. They dressed like most of their generation. Both wore faded tattered jeans. I will never understand that. Their jeans looked like they had been through years of hard service, handed down from an earlier owner. The truth was that they had probably been bought in that condition. Vivian wore a tank top. Her long hair was braided and hung to one side. A headband kept everything in place. The boy wore a hooded T-shirt, which was in bad need of a washing. A baseball cap emblazed with the emblem of the Yankees was worn backward on his head. This was another thing I just don't get. Before the tour was over, the boy was holding his hand over his eyes to block the sun—wasn't that what the hat's bill was supposed to do? Well anyway, the boy marched to the back of the bus with Vivian trying to catch up. She gently pleaded, "Wait for me, babe!" That was all that Luka needed. For the rest of the tour, this boy would be "Babe."

There was plenty of room to spread out; still, Luka encouraged us to sit close to the front so we could hear the commentary. The Wisconsin family sat in the second row, on both sides of the bus, so that the children each had a window seat. Babe and Vivian remained in the last row.

"Good afternoon, everyone! Again, my name is Luka, and I am going to be your guide for today's tour." Luka went on, "Please excuse my accent. I have been in your country for more than ten years now. My English is very good, yes? So okay, I will be telling you about all the wonderful sights that we visit. Please, ask questions. I might have to make something up, but I promise to give an answer." I was pretty sure that I knew more than he did about the monuments of Washington, but I remained quiet. No need to be an ugly tourist, not today.

"Hey, Luka. Is there any music on this bus?" Babe was shouting from the back of the bus.

"Well, I know some songs that I can sing—some in English and some in Greek. Would that work?"

A disappointing response was quick in coming. "Nah, we're good."

With that out of the way, Luka started our tour. "You on the right, look inside. See him sitting up there in that big chair? I watch him sit up there almost every day. I am wondering, 'What is he thinking as he sits there?'"

Again, there was noise from the back of the bus, "He's not thinking anything. He's a rock!"

I couldn't help myself. I shot back a rather stern, "Come on, kid, give the guy a break!" I just knew this kid was going to be trouble.

Babe decided to play Luka's game, "Okay, I got it. How about, 'Is there anyone sneaking up behind me?'"

"That's mean but funny." Vivian was at least awake.

RB wasn't the least bit shy. He shouted, "I wish they had moved my chair closer to the front so I could look out over the river."

Luka was not going to be outdone. He said, "I think Lincoln was a fair man. He is thinking, Poor Washington, they built me this beautiful building and all he got was that giant pencil over there."

Almost on cue, the bus added her voice to the conversation with something like, *clank…clank…sputter…sputter…*

Luka started muttering under his breath. Not so quiet that we couldn't hear him, "Come on, old bus. These nice people have paid for us to show them the town. I know clank, and I know sputter, no problem, just start moving." I must tell you; I was thinking that Bethany's walking shoes were going to come in handy on this tour.

The bus pulled away from the curb and slowly started making its way along a well-traveled tour route. Luka began the official tour with, "Okay, friends, here we go. There are some roads closed today, so we will visit the monuments in backward order."

Robin asked the first question. It was silly, but it helped get the tour off to a good start. "What was that?" Luka asked. "Hey, I'm going to like you. No, you face forward, of course, you can sit any way you like. It is the monuments that will be backward. More correctly, they will be forward too, just in reverse order. For those with a map, we will start with Arlington National Cemetery instead of the Vietnam Veteran's Memorial."

The bus shook a little but continued to move along the backside of Lincoln's monument. "Friends, I have a question for you. How many were the states of the US when Lincoln was president?" Luka was big on group participation.

Robin was in the conversation again. "Thirty!" she shouted, sure that she was right.

One of the Florida wives spoke up next, "No, dear, I think there were more. I believe there were thirty-four states following the civil war."

"Yeah, I'll go with that," Babe was awake and continuing to be the sore spot in the group. "She was probably around back then."

I turned around and glared at the kid. This fellow was going to be trouble.

"Well," Luka said, "just count the columns around the memorial. There is one for each state." Then he added, "You should get thirty-six."

The bus surged forward, and the group started crossing the river. Luka described the giant statues called the Arts of War that stood on either side of the bridge. "We have many beautiful statues like these in Europe. They remind me of home."

It was the bus's turn to speak again. *Clank...clank...sputter... sputter*, again came from somewhere under the hood.

"What is your problem today?" Luka's earlier mumble was now a low, but audible, question to the bus. "Neither of us is getting any younger, but I am hoping we can both finish today without some problems. Please...just keep going."

The tour group made it safely across the bridge, through the roundabout, and up to the gate of Arlington National Cemetery when the bus made a final complaint. "Clank I know, sputter I know, but what is pop! Oh, come on, old bus, don't do this." Luka was pleading much louder. It was clear that responding was well beyond the bus's abilities.

Luka talked to his bus as if it could talk back, "Come on, bus! I just told these nice people you were going to be fine. I don't want to make them think I do not tell the truth. More popping, what is this popping? No. No, no, no! You can't stop here. So, you are stopping here? Now, what am I going to do?" I had been on sick buses before; this one sounded like it had gone as far as it was going to go.

Every voice on the bus came to life. Each voice masked the cries of the next. It was hard to make out a single question, but there was no doubt what was being asked. What was going to happen now? How would we get back to the Lincoln Memorial? Would we get our money back? I have no doubt that Luka heard all of these and more. He heard anger coming from the back of the bus, and he knew that he needed to do something—fast.

"Well, friends, as you can see the bus wants to take a rest." Luka's voice was calm like he had been here before. "I'll tell you what, I am going to add a walking tour to your agenda for free. How many of you have been on a walking tour of the National Cemetery?" I was right about this being the end of the line for the bus. What's more, I could have sold Bethany's walking shoes for a pretty penny right then.

"Hey, man, I didn't sign up to walk!" The unhappy voice of the teenage boy was once again bellowing from the back of the bus.

I had a couple of suggestions for Babe, but before I could offer them up, Luka replied in a calm, gentle tone and all the time smiling, "Well, you are free to stay on the bus, but it will be a shame if you missed what's inside of those gates."

The tour group left the bus with a mix of emotions. The Wisconsin family bounded off the bus, embarking on a great adventure. It was easy to see that the teenagers were the least excited.

Luka handed water bottles to each of us and headed off in the direction of the big iron gates. Shouting over his shoulder, Luka said, "This is a very big place, so stay together. If you get lost, ask someone how to find the Women's Memorial. We will go back to the bus from there."

I tried to be a good sport, but I also knew that Bethany and I had other plans for the afternoon. I mustered up the most civil tone that I owned and asked, "How long are we going to be here?"

Luka had already thought about that. Given the time of day, and the need to let the bus rest, he said that two hours should be right.

"I promise you will need to come back later, but we will do our best to see the really important sites in two hours." I could see that Luka was hoping that we would accept this new plan without too much fuss.

We entered the gates and followed Luka as he turned right and started down the paved road. Luka started the walk as if this was a planned part of the day. "General facts. Let me tell you some general things about this cemetery. It covers over 650 acres and has more than 400,000 gravesites. It is huge. The Union Army seized the land from Robert E. Lee at the start of the civil war, and it started to serve as a cemetery soon after." He boasted that he could reel off hundreds of other facts, but then offered just one more. "There are war dead here from all the way back to the American Revolutionary War, and there are several non-Americans buried here too."

Unlike some in the group, Robin was paying attention. "Wait a minute. If the cemetery started during the civil war, where did the people from the American Revolutionary War come from?" That was a smart question.

Luka was glad to show off his cemetery trivia. "Well, those bodies were moved here early in the twentieth century. And before you ask, I am not sure how many foreign soldiers are buried here, but I do know that there are gravesites for men from China, Australia, Canada, and four from my country, Greece."

"Anyone know how many American presidents are buried here?" Luka seemed sure the group would know there was at least one.

Multiple voices said, "Two."

Luka had expected most of the group would know that John F. Kennedy's gravesite was there, but would they know the other president? I am sure that he didn't want to embarrass anyone, so he went on, "Of course, you know that William Howard Taft is here as is John F. Kennedy. Now if you will stay together for just a couple more minutes, we will be at President Taft's gravesite."

There was a change coming over our little group. Each step into the cemetery seemed to quiet everyone. At first, people walked with their heads high, like they were bird watching. Every block we walked had a thousand graves, every block slowed our steps and lowered our eyes closer to the ground.

We reached the first stop on the cemetery tour, and Luka gathered everyone together. It was amazing. Without a cue card or guidebook, he commenced reciting a list of impressive facts about this long-dead president. He was finishing with President Taft being the only president to serve as chief justice of the Supreme Court when he glanced at his watch and insisted that we move onto the next stop. "We must get there on time. We must move along," he shouted. Increasing the volume caused his voice to squeak and brought muffled laughter from the children.

Vivian thought that women should get some equal time on this tour, "What about first ladies? Are there any first ladies buried here?"

Her question seemed to surprise Luka, but while continuing to press on to the next stopping point, he said, "Yes, there are two. Mrs. Taft is buried next to her husband, right over there. The second you will see at our next stop. Am I going too fast? Sorry, we can't be late, so please keep up." He was beginning to take on the character of the white rabbit from *Alice in Wonderland*.

Luka's pace was far from a casual walk in the park. He was aware that some members of the group needed a kinder march, but he did not want to be late. The Wisconsin kids were really enjoying this forced march that Luka was taking us on. Rachael kept reminding them to drink water and not run ahead. They drank water as they took up a pace short of running.

Only a couple minutes passed when Luka started gathering his little group into a tight circle. "See," he said, "isn't this beautiful?" Luka continued, "President Kennedy was originally buried over there, to the north just below the Arlington House."

"Why did they move him?" Bethany had been silent until then. I was surprised that she did not remember why he was moved. We had taken a tour of the cemetery once before, but it was many years ago.

Luka was loving this chance to be a real tour guide. "Well, so many people wanted to visit the president's grave that they needed a bigger spot. It took some time to get everything completed, so about four years later, Mr. Kennedy was moved to this spot. This eternal flame was lit, and it has burned ever since."

"And there," he said, "is where the other first lady is buried. You know, she married one of my countrymen a few years after President Kennedy was assassinated. Yep, Mrs. Jacqueline Kennedy Onassis, that was her name. Onassis is Greek you know." There was a pause, and then he added, "But you know, I am American now."

"Please, we must hurry." Luka was pleading as he watched the hands advance on his watch. "Take all the pictures you want but walk as you do. We have only ten minutes."

"Hey, wait a minute!" It was Babe again. "I thought you were hurrying us to get here. What's the rush?"

Luka started explaining as they moved up the hill. "The changing of the guard at the Tomb of the Unknown Soldier is in ten minutes. Either we hurry, or we wait thirty minutes for the next one."

Our group followed the road to where it turned to the right. We turned in the opposite direction, taking a path leading directly to the final stopping point on the tour.

As we neared the tomb, Luka began explaining what we would see and how we must behave. Luka was very careful with his words. "Friends, this is a very solemn place. You must be respectful."

Luka was more familiar with this place than anyone would have thought. "Friends, the first time I came to this place, I was very confused. I mean why are there guards here? Not just guards, but soldiers—serious-looking men with guns having knives on the end. They marched back and forth in front of this big marble monument like it was full of gold."

He continued, "They couldn't be worried about those inside the tomb getting out. I don't want to disrespect the dead, but they weren't going to escape. And, why would someone want to break in? This was very strange"

Without being asked, I said, "The soldiers inside this tomb died protecting our country. They died, and no one knows who they were. The guards are showing the deep respect of a nation for these brave unknown men." I must tell you; it was all I could do to fight back tears as I thought about those men and others like them.

Luka continued, "This tomb contains the remains of one soldier from World War I, World War II, the Korean War, and the Vietnam War." Luka wasn't exactly right about that, but I wasn't going to challenge him.

"It's starting!" whispered Luka.

"Psst. Everyone count the steps of the guard as he moves back and forth," Luka obviously was trying to make a point.

"Great, now he's giving us homework." This was a voice loud enough to be heard over the crowd. Babe had missed Luka's instruction to remain respectful and couldn't see the point in the show anyway. I'm ashamed to tell you that I lost control. I guess it was instinct, but I grabbed the front of that kid's T-shirt, stared him directly in the eyes, and dared him to make another sound. The boy was younger than this relic from years gone by, but he was pretty sure that I was prepared to slap him upside of this head. I may be old, but I promise you that I would have come out the better of the two if it had come to that.

Three soldiers executed a "changing of the guard" ceremony exactly like it had been done for decades—never altered once. Every eye, even those of the rowdy teen, remained fixed on the guards as they performed with machinelike precision. The ceremony ended with a single soldier watching over the tomb.

Luka was beaming. You would have thought that he was one of the guards. "I promised you this would be special. Was I right?" There was no doubt; he was right—our bobbing heads were all the proof that was needed to the question.

Now comes the part that fixed the visit to Arlington in my memory; Luka led the group a few paces away from the tomb and then began replaying the entire scene to us. Suddenly coming to attention, he began to march and count aloud. "One, two, three... eighteen, nineteen, someone tell me when I shall stop?"

The Wisconsin kids were ready. In tandem, they shouted, "Twenty-one!"

"Twenty, twenty-one...right." Luka finished the first pass of the guard's movement. "Then what?"

Babe was sure that Luka's question was dumb. So, he shouted, "You turn around and go back of course. Anybody could figure that out."

Luka did not turn; instead, he held his hand in the air, wagging his index finger back and forth. "Sorry, that's not right."

"The guard paused after the twenty-first step and waited exactly twenty-one seconds." It was clear that Luka had practiced this routine before, and he began to count aloud, "One, two, three.... And then he turned around and marched back." Babe seemed positive he had it right this time.

"Eighteen, nineteen, twenty, twenty-one…no, I'm sorry you missed something. You see, the guard turned toward the tomb and paused. And guess what, he paused again for twenty-one seconds." Once again Luka started counting out loud.

"So, let me guess. After he got to twenty-one, he turned and waited twenty-one more seconds before he returned. Right?" It looked like Babe was beginning to soften to Luka's technique and was hoping to finally be right for once.

"Exactly!" Luka was about to make a new friend. "And when the guard returns the twenty-one steps, he repeats the twenty-one-second pause and turns before starting all over again."

"I was about to say that." The boy's response encouraged Luka to go on.

I thought, *If only you could teach him how to wear a hat.*

"Twenty-one steps, twenty-one seconds, it is twenty-one that will help you know the honor being given by these soldiers."

Luka was about to deliver the final point in the lesson. "I know that all of you have heard of a twenty-one-gun salute. All over the world, it is the highest honor given to anyone. Every step and every pause of the guard was delivering the highest honor possible from our thankful country."

"I get it," said Vivian. "This is awesome."

I just smiled at her. "I will call you Biscuit if you like."

More smiles were exchanged among the group.

Luka again displayed his impressive knowledge of the tomb. He went on and on about the guards. He told us that guards had protected the tomb since before most of us were born—I wondered if he meant me. He told us that they guarded the tomb in the blazing hot sun, during blizzards, and hurricanes—only a direct order from the president could keep a guard from honoring these heroes. He went on about the guards carefully spending hours every day making uniforms perfect, cutting their hair every day, memorizing the history of the cemetery and those buried there. He made the point that these guards were special soldiers representing every one of us to the unknown heroes who died protecting our freedom.

The mood of the group changed. The pace back down the hill was slower, and our eyes were scanning tombstones, reading names, and taking note of the ages of those buried beneath the stone. Many were not much older than the teenage couple that was part of our band.

Luka had not forgotten that the bus was not at its best when they arrived at the cemetery. He began to talk sweetly to the bus as if it was an old friend rather than a collection of nuts and bolts. "Okay, bus, I'm back, and you have had your rest. It's time to get these nice people on their way. Are you ready? That's a good bus. Now behave yourself until we get back."

Luka turned his attention back to us. "All right, my good people, let's see what else we can see before it gets dark. You know, the Jefferson Memorial is most beautiful at sunset. We'll take some time there for pictures."

"Are you hungry? There're good food trucks in the parking lot. I know you'll want to share your money with some of those nice people. I can promise that my friend Juan will have the most excellent tacos and falafels."

"Hey, Luka." The voice came from far in the back of the bus.

"Yes, how can I help?" Luka didn't seem sure that he wanted to hear this request.

"Thanks for taking us through the cemetery." Then he added, "Is there any music on this bus?"

Luka smiled and without missing a beat said, "Okay, folks, here is a tune that my momma sang to me when I was a small boy in Greece. Sing along if you know the words."

* * * * *

Out the Book and Into the Street

Uncle Jeb refused to forget the sacrifice his younger brother made. He told me stories about when both Nathan and he were wading through the rice paddies in body-pounding rain, eating tasteless food from a tin can, and sleeping with one eye open, so I am sure that Uncle Jeb was familiar with the sacrifices of many others. He never fails to stand for the flag or cry on Memorial Day. He hoped that no more children would go off to war and that the children would never forget those who did. Can you understand what Uncle Jeb was thinking? How can you show appreciation for those who have or are serving to protect this country?

DAVID, RETURNING HOME

Last summer, Aunt Elizabeth's son came to the family's Independence Day celebration. The Marinos have been gathering for that celebration for as long as I can remember. David Jr. had just come back from selling the family home. Both Aunt Elizabeth and Uncle David were gone. David Jr. lived a long way away from the family home, so selling it made sense. David seemed to need some time to relax and think. The July 4 family gathering probably wasn't the best place for quiet time or thinking, but by the time David left, he seemed in better spirits. I will let him tell you his story about returning to his childhood home.

*****

I am sure that the neighbors took me for a stranger or maybe a realtor when I pulled into the driveway. Most of the people on the block were new to the area, but there were a few that if they looked closely would recognize me. I am sure that Mrs. Delgado would say, "Why, Junior, how you have grown." Yes, they would remember me as Junior.

Junior was the nickname used by everyone when I was younger. My colleagues know me as Dr. David Bates, or just Dr. Bates; no one would call me Junior. As for the doctor part, I'm not a "make you feel better" doctor. You would probably call me a "I don't understand a thing you are saying" doctor. That's because I'm an astrobiology scientist. There is no simple way to explain what I do. Those who heard my parents brag about me would probably say that I was the guy who was looking for ET. Kinder people would say that I studied life from other planets. I like to explain that I focus on theories about extraterrestrial life, but somehow everyone always ends up wanting to talk about ET or *The X Files*.

It would have been easy to mistake me for a realtor; there was a "For Sale" sign in the front yard, and I was dressed in a dark suit. If I had been in my work clothes, I would have been in a white lab coat or maybe a polo shirt and shorts. The dark suit was because I had just come from my mother's funeral.

My mother, whom everyone called Lizzy, passed away the week before. Her death was not unexpected. She was eighty-four and had a small list of ailments but a long list of medicines that had become part of her daily routine. In the end, she enjoyed a full life. The few old friends that remained, family members, and people from the community celebrated her life in a very grand way.

Lizzy, whose real name was Elizabeth, was born and raised on a farm in northeast Tennessee. She loved being on the farm and planned to return to the area when she graduated from college. My mom was bright. She won a scholarship to a college in Indiana where she studied animal husbandry—the perfect study for someone planning to return to the farm.

Mom met Dave Bates Senior, my dad, while in college. Dad was from central Indiana and dedicated to becoming a civil engineer. He wanted to build cites and superhighways. Dad's and Mom's stories are like those of a lot of college kids. They studied hard, fell in love, graduated, and got married. This is where Mom's plans changed.

Dad was offered a job in Lexington, Kentucky, with a large engineering company. The job had great potential and a handsome salary. It was too good for a young, married couple to pass up, so Dad and Mom packed up and moved to Kentucky. The move meant that Mom had to put her plans to return to Tennessee on hold.

Life happens, and before long, Mom was expecting me. I was born several months after that, and thoughts of returning to Tennessee faded further into the future.

Dad worked hard, making a good life for us. We moved into a beautiful home just before my second birthday. I was standing in the front yard of that house, preparing to sell it after all those years.

Dad moved up in the company, put some new initials behind his name, and was on the way to being one of the very best engineers in the company. Then something happened. Somewhere between graduate school and his fortieth birthday, Dad developed a new passion. It started when he was invited to be a guest speaker for a college engineering course, and it grew from there. In less than a year, my dad resigned from his corporate job and assumed a teaching position at the university. He remained one of the most respected professors in the engineering department until his retirement.

Dad and Mom were happy together after his retirement, doing all the things that retired couples hope to do. They traveled to see places that they had long hoped to see but never had time. When at home, Dad spent most mornings making sure that every blade of his Kentucky bluegrass was perfectly manicured and edged. A picture of his handiwork could have served as the front cover of *Home and Garden Magazine*.

Dad passed away in 2010 leaving Mom to carry on alone. It was easy to see that Mom missed Dad terribly, but she had a strength that propelled her forward. That didn't mean that she had the same priorities as Dad. She was less attentive to the yard. She wasn't seeking any awards for the straightest edges or smoothest lawn in town. A gardener was hired in short order so she could spend time on other passions. While Mom wasn't the groundskeeper that Dad was, she never lost her love for growing things.

Mom was appointed a Kentucky Colonel about the time that I left for college. If you don't know, a Kentucky Colonel has nothing to do with the army or fighting. Rather, it is the highest honor that the governor of Kentucky can bestow on a person. Mom's certificate said that it was for "noteworthy accomplishments and outstanding service." I don't suppose anyone knows why the governor chose to appoint her to the Kentucky Colonels—I'm not sure Mom knew—but she took the appointment as her calling. Mom poured herself into volunteering her time. She filled her week with planting gardens and tutoring children.

Only death could stop her from serving, and that is what happened. A neighbor went to check on her the Wednesday before I went home and found that she had passed away. It appeared that it happened earlier the evening before. The light was on at the table beside her favorite chair, a cup of cold tea sat on the table beside her, and her favorite book of Robert Frost's poems lay on her lap open to the one that she most often read. Mom had underlined the entire first stanza of the poem.

> I shall be telling this with a sigh.
> Somewhere ages and ages hence:
> Two roads diverged in a wood, and I,
> I took the one less traveled by,
> And that has made all the difference.

This was my first trip to the house since the funeral. I was too busy making arrangements. I was supposed to meet a realtor to walk through the house and complete the required paperwork, but before the meeting, I wanted to take a few minutes to wander around. I knew that selling the house was the right thing to do, but it was going to be hard.

I started surveying the property by crossing the front yard and moving around the east side of the house. I had the strangest sensation. I wasn't Dr. Bates, space explorer. I was just Junior standing on the well-manicured lawn. I was tempted to pull my shoes off and feel the lush green grass under my feet. I remembered when my dad planted the lilacs that still stood up against the house. They were much bigger now. I was surprised when I turned the corner of the house. My old treehouse was still up in that old hickory tree. Dad said that he was going to tear it down years ago, but there it was, almost exactly as it had been when I was eight years old. I remembered how hard Dad worked to secure the platforms to the trunk of the hickory tree. Dad said, "This treehouse is as strong as any building I designed." He must have been right because there it still was.

I spent hour upon hour in that treehouse on summer afternoons and late at night. It was my favorite thinking spot and the main meeting place for our small gang of future explorers—the mountains of Tibet and jungles of South America were our normal destinations.

I wondered why the treehouse was still there and if it would help the resale of the house. Silly I know. I guess I had outgrown dreams of Tibetan mountains and South American jungles.

I could see directly into the kitchen from the east side of the house. I gazed in, remembering the image of my mother standing there and the shape of a small boy at the counter behind her. That boy had such plans. I could hear the conversation going on in there. The boy was going to travel down the Amazon in search of lost treasure. The boy was almost certainly holding the most recent copy of *National Geographic* or *Boy's Life* magazine. With a backpack full of peanut butter sandwiches and a sharp machete, he was going to chop his way through that dense forest and discover treasures left by the ancient Incas. The money earned from the Inca treasure was going to help pay for him and his explorer friends' travels into Tibet to look for yetis. Yes, sir, old memories came flooding into his mind. I wondered if any of those boys ever made it to Tibet. Whatever happened to that small band of boys and their dreams?

I made my way around to the back. Things were exactly as they should have been. There was a large brick barbeque that Dad had built when I was small. I couldn't remember a time when it was not there. Dozens of family gatherings were known to those bricks. Fourth of Julys, birthdays, and Labor Day celebrations were just a few reasons for family gatherings. My memories didn't go back as far here as they did for the treehouse. In these memories, my explorer friends and I were older. We were no less committed to seeing the world and no less distracted by Emily Fisher and her ever-present gang of four—all through high school those girls were together. The girls thought all the talk about Inca's treasure and bigfoot was foolishness. College was quickly approaching, and they were focused on their futures. How could anyone depend on fortune-hunting to live? I insisted that Inca treasure remained undiscovered, but in my mind, I somehow knew that Emily was at least a little right. Back in the present, I stood there wondering what happened to Emily and her gang of four.

I slid the key into the lock on the backdoor only to find that it was not locked—Mom often forgot to lock that door. I made my way in and stood in the hallway that led to the front of the house. I could not believe it. It had been a few years since I was home, but nothing had changed. There were hooks on the wall for jackets and hats. I can tell you that I wasn't surprised to see Dad's old gardening hat where it always stayed on the second hook. Dad had placed it there the last time he came in from working in the yard—perhaps having just trimmed that overgrown lilac bush.

I was surprised by how familiar the smells were. These were not the aroma of something baking or Mom's perfume. They were smells that cook into a house over time. They are hard to explain, but when they meet your nose, they identify the home more clearly than the numbers on the mailbox.

I wandered into the room, which was the evening gathering place, the den. There were two very worn, very comfortable chairs turned so that they half-faced the fireplace and half-faced a large picture window. One of these chairs was where Mom had spent her last evening. Her last night was not the memory that replayed on the little screen inside my head. No, this memory was older.

I remembered coming home from college at Christmastime, my freshman year. Yes, Junior went off to college fully forgetting Inca treasure. My goal was to complete college and program computers. I possessed strong mathematic abilities and liked problem-solving. I didn't know exactly what I would do with computers, but back then, everyone wanted to work with computers.

Dad had other ideas. "Junior," he said, "you don't have the temperament for that kind of work." Dad was right, but I was unwilling to hear any challenge to my plans, regardless of how valid they might be. I remembered shouting, something like, "I know better than you," or at least something close to that and seeing the disappointment on Dad's face. Still, I determined to stay the course, perhaps more so because of my dad's objections—that's what happens when you are young. I returned to college after Christmas break and enrolled in computer science courses. But the den, oh the den. Erase those few moments, and I would remember the hours that were spent in the den. It is strange to me now that of all the talks and laughing that had gone on in that room, I remembered that encounter with my dad.

I was vindicated in the den a year or so later. There standing next to the sofa, I announced that I had a job with a large computer firm in Colorado. Starting pay was good, and I was going to be doing exciting things with computers and airplanes.

It was then that I was certain that I was not alone. There were no creaking floors or bumping sounds, but I was certain that someone was there.

I stood quiet for a few moments when I heard a familiar voice. "I was right you know." It was my dad's voice. I turned to see him sitting in his chair, holding the newspaper.

I am a scientist, and I explore life beyond this planet. Still, I was taken back. I reasoned that I was suffering some shock from the death of my mother. I must be seeing things.

"Then again, you were right too." Dad was continuing to make his point. "How long did that computer job last?"

"Not that long," I was talking to a ghost or something that I was imagining. My training was trying to process what was happening and looking for a logical answer. While that was going on, I had to admit that I didn't know what I was going to be doing with that computer job. The job was in Colorado and the company was working with the airlines, but not with airplanes. I was there less than two years when I knew I hated what I was doing. It would have been better to search for treasure where there was no treasure than keep doing this.

"And how are things going now?" I was having a conversation with someone who had been gone for eight years. Dad didn't have an "I told you so" tone. It was an honest question, seeking an honest answer.

Whatever was happening, this was my dad, and I was welcoming this conversation. "Well, part of it you remember." I quit that job and moved back home to think through what was going to happen next. I moved back into my old room where not a thing had been changed. I spent days trying to decide what to do. "You must know some of it. There is more since you…I mean since you, uh"

"Died?" My dad never was one to beat around the bush.

"Well, yes."

Dad surely remembered talking in this room. Back then, he said, "Junior, you need to go back to school and get a graduate degree. Use what you have learned to move to the next level."

I had learned that I had no interest in writing computer programs to make it easier to buy airplane tickets. I needed something more, so I agreed that going back to school was a good choice, but to do what?

It is funny how I discovered my next career move. Dad and I were sitting downstairs watching television—which we seldom did. Suddenly I was hearing full voice on the TV, William Shatner's voice announced, "Space the final frontier, our mission…"

Space, I thought. I could hunt for treasure, in space. I already understood computers, marry that to space science, and who knows what I could find. Dad did not argue this time. Maybe the memory of the last time we tried talking through my plans was still floating in the air. No shouting, only encouraging words were exchanged; now the rest is history.

One of my courses introduced me to the idea of other life in the universe. The explorer in me tingled as I began to consider that we might not be alone. I could not rid my mind of the question, "Who or what else is out there?"

I finished the program but still hungered to know more about what was not known. I couldn't leave school just yet. There were answers to questions that I didn't have yet. I stayed and stayed, looking for the answers. In time, I received a doctorate, and I still did not have answers. No answers, but I had the tools to begin exploring for answers. And that is how Junior became Dr. David Bates.

Turning my conversation back to my dad, I said, "I am very happy. Every day is a day to explore what were only little dots to me as a boy. I don't know if I will ever find anything, but the hunt drives me onward. You know, I have found several planets that could support life as we know it. Someone out there could be looking up into their sky at us—wondering if we are out there."

Dad replies with two short phrases, "Good answer. I'm proud of you."

I stood there speechless for several minutes. I heard something else and turned to see what it was. I didn't find anything, and when I turned back, my dad was gone. The scientist in me wanted to analyze the encounter. Junior was just glad to have had the time.

I continued to wander around the house and continued to remember growing up within those walls. Thinking about Mom, Dad, and me, I was surprised how different and yet how similar our lives were. Each of us started with a plan, a passion. Each of us abandoned the plan for something else—something better and something out of view. Mom traded a farm for a family and the life that came with it. Dad traded shaping high-rise buildings and large highways for shaping engineers who would do greater things. And me, I traded exploring the jungle for exploring the universe.

I started humming a little tune that my mother liked. Mom thought it was an old Italian song. It didn't matter. The main line of the song was, "Que sera sera, whatever will be will be." No doubt about it, life is strange. On the one hand, we set goals and work hard to reach them. Good goals, even goals that are bigger than us. And while chasing those goals or even achieving them, life moves us in a different direction. For a minute, it almost seems better to not set a goal in the first place. Of course, as an astrobiologist, I know that you don't change the direction of something unless it is moving—you go nowhere sitting still. All my family's goals had a part in getting me to where I was. Yep, that's the way life is. We set one course, and life blows us in a different direction. Whether a large change or several small ones, we still find ourselves someplace other than where we thought we were going. Most times, it is right where we were supposed to be.

* * * * *

Out of the Book and Into the Street

Just as Junior noted, "We set one course, and life blows us in a different direction." This is true for more people than you think. A recent poll of college students revealed that freshmen entering college are likely to change their major twice before graduation. If that happens in just four years, imagine what happens over a lifetime. Take time to find out from family members how their lives may be different from what they planned. Write down your goals for the future, and put it someplace special so that you can come back to it later.

ANTONIO, THE FALL OF SAIGON

There are so many great stories about the family, but I must admit this one from Antonio is one of the greatest. When Antonio shows up at family dinners, the children always ask him to tell them about when he was in the war. He has so many adventures to talk about, but why do children always want to hear war stories? I'm sure that it must be because Antonio's stories contain snakes and monkeys, bombs, and other stuff. He paints the jungle and the people in the mind of listeners so that the listeners can almost feel the monsoon rain on their face. Most times the stories are exciting and funny. The story that I am going to let him tell is different. It ends with Antonio just sitting quietly, appearing to have gone to another place and time. While the story seems to make him sad, he is willing to tell it with very little prompting.

Antonio will tell you that he entered the air force at the very bottom of its ranks. He enlisted in the air force after high school. He had no intention serving more than four years, but he didn't know what he wanted to do or what he wanted to be, so he would have four years to figure it out. He went on to be commissioned as an officer and continued to raise in the ranks. It was more than two decades before he decided to leave the air force.

It only took the air force a week or so to figure out what the family knew all along. Antonio was very bright—we say gifted. He finished basic training, finished language training, and was in Vietnam before anyone knew what had happened. Antonio never talks about what he did. Most of his stories are about people he met or places he visited. Still, we know he was very brave—by the time he retired, he had medals as proof.

Antonio served in Vietnam during the last four years of the war. I said the last four years. Remember he was only going to stay four years? Well, during the last year of his enlistment, he decided that he wanted to stay longer. It turns out that his four years stretched to more than twenty by the time he retired.

Antonio flew on a reconnaissance airplane all the time he was in Vietnam. We call it a "spy plane" when he starts telling his stories, which makes him shake his head or his eyes roll. He tries to correct us, but the stories are so much better when we say "spy plane." He has pictures of the airplanes he flew on. These help with our claims of "spy plane" since some of the planes look different. The picture the children like best is one that has a long black nose; they think it looks like Charlie Brown's dog Snoopy with wings.

I am so proud of Antonio. I could talk about him for hours, but it is better if I let him talk for himself, so let's have Antonio tell his story.

* * * * *

It was late April 1975. North and South Vietnam were still at war. Most of the Americans had left Vietnam, and the war was going badly for South Vietnam. The North Vietnamese army had crossed into South Vietnam and was marching south toward the capital, Saigon, and there was no one to stop them. There were still some American soldiers and State Department staff left in Saigon. They were directly in the path of the advancing army. Our government launched an emergency mission to evacuate the remaining Americans from the country. They called it Operation Frequent Wind. Don't ask where the name came from, that is just a military thing.

The plan was to evacuate Americans citizens, some Vietnamese citizens, and all remaining military from Saigon. They were using anything that could fly or float to get people out of the country. Our squadron was ordered to protect them as they left. One of our primary tasks was to make sure that the ambassador made it to safety.

"Operation Frequent Wind" demanded that my unit fly non-stop for the last ten days of April. We were flying from Okinawa,

Japan, so my crew flew twenty-two hours straight for each mission. After returning from a mission, I would have twelve hours to rest and then get back into the airplane for another twenty-two hours. The flights were so long that our plane had to refuel twice in the air. Can you imagine a flying gas station? Our airplane would pull up to the flying gas station where the gas station would let out a hose and fill up our tanks. It was sort of like getting gas in your car except that the gas station and the airplane were speeding along at two hundred miles per hour, five miles above the ground. After loading four thousand gallons into our tanks, we returned to work—they never checked the oil or cleaned the windshield.

A day in the air and a half day to rest, this continued over a week. Late on Tuesday, April 29, we flew the final "Frequent Wind" mission. By the time this mission was over, each crew member would have more than 160 hours of flight time for just a seven-day period. We might have been tired, but our training and the importance of what we were doing kept us awake, clear-headed. We were exhausted after that final day, but we could have gone on longer; people depended on us. But April 30 was the last day.

Our crew arrived off the coast of Vietnam long before the sun came up on Wednesday. There was another plane there waiting for our arrival so they could go home for some much-needed sleep.

Things were getting worse in the city of Saigon. The North Vietnamese army was getting closer, and people were fleeing Saigon. Planes, packed with families who left everything, flew to safety in Thailand. Some just flew as far as they could and crashed into rice fields. Boats set course for the ships off the coast. How they left was not as important as leaving.

Helicopters were everywhere. They couldn't fly as far and might not hold as many people as an airplane, but they could do something that airplanes could not, land on ships. There were several Navy ships off the coast of Vietnam where they could land. The helicopters gathered a load of people from the city, flew out to the ships, dropped off the people, and returned for another group. There were so many helicopters that when I looked out the window of the plane, it looked like a line of ants moving from a picnic to an ant mound, and this was no picnic. I could see rockets rising from the ground aimed at the helicopters. I had seen rockets and missiles launched before, along with bursts of artillery fire, but those were when one army was attacking another, and both could fight back. The helicopters were carrying businessmen, farmers, and their families fleeing in unarmed helicopters. They were helpless to defend themselves. There was nothing that could be done to help those fleeing except pray.

I was responsible to protect the military helicopters that were ferrying people from the city to ships awaiting them offshore. My job, keep them as far from danger as possible. These helicopters were better off than those poor folks trying to escape. They had guns to protect themselves.

Today, protecting these helicopters was even more important. These helicopters were responsible for getting the last of the marines and the ambassador out of the embassy. This would be the final day of "Frequent Wind" and fighting for American soldiers.

"Lady Lace 09, inbound at 0458." Years later, I remember the call sign of the helicopter and the time. I flew over a hundred times in and around Vietnam. I don't remember much about those flights, there is even less I want to say about them, but I remember that call sign. Lady Lace 09 was the navy helicopter that was supposed to pick up the last of the marines and the ambassador. At 0458, it was two minutes until five o'clock in the morning. The sun was not up. No sun yet, that was good. Lady Lace 09 would have an easier time getting into the compound where the marines were waiting.

Lady Lace 09 was not alone. Besides my crew, others helped keep the helicopter safe. I heard chatter coming from a gunship that was flying in the area. This was an AC-130, we called it Spooky, others called it Puff, like Puff the Magic Dragon. It got that name because of a cannon it carried. The gun could launch 1,800 bullets in a single minute. Think about it, *One Mississippi, two Mississippi, three Mississippi.* Before you finish your third Mississippi, one hundred bullets would be fired. Spooky was deadly accurate—the pilot could write his name on the ground with his cannon as easily as you can write your name in the sand with a stick. Lady Lace 09 was in good hands.

Lady Lace 09 landed safely, but the pilot reported that there was a problem. Ambassador Martin did not want to leave yet. There were still a couple of hundred Vietnamese citizens that he hoped to help get out of the country.

The problem was quickly solved. The marines had different orders. They were ordered to get the ambassador onto the helicopter, even if that meant handcuffing him. Resistance was futile. The marines were going to protect him right onto Lady Lace 09, and that was the end of that.

In the meantime, streams of helicopters were arriving at the navy's ship anchored off the coast. This time, they were making one-way trips. There were so many that the ship's crew would unload a helicopter and then push the helicopter into the sea. People were more important than machinery. A group would land, a helicopter would go over the side of the ship, and another group would land. No one knows how many helicopters are resting on the bottom of the South China Sea.

Lady Lace 09 took off from the compound and flew directly toward the waiting navy ship. As it crossed the shoreline and over water, Lady Lace 09 sent out a radio message to all that were listening; it simply said, "Tiger, Tiger, Tiger." I heard these words and knew it was over. It was the signal that the ambassador was on board and that they had left Vietnam. In a few short minutes, Ambassador Martin was ushered onto a waiting navy ship and then returned to the United States. His work in Saigon was done, so was the work of the US military. The war was over, and we had not won.

I will end with a little piece of trivia, World War II trivia. In December of 1941, the Japanese attacked the US port at Pearl Harbor. This attack started the war between Japan and the United States. Do you know the message that the Japanese used to start the attack on Pearl Harbor? My guess is that you don't. It was "*Tora! Tora! Tora!*" The English translation of that is the words, "Tiger! Tiger! Tiger!"

* * * * *

Out the Book and Into the Street

Antonio is like many veterans. They experienced much, some they can tell, some they won't. Regardless of where or when they served, all deserve our appreciation. How can you show your appreciation to even one of these brave men and women? Maybe there is one you're thinking of right now.

TERRANCE, FIGHTING WITH THE REBELS

As the story keeper, I have stories that go back as far as there are people to remember them. This comes from many years ago. My mother's father, Terrance, was called T. O. by everyone. He was born in 1880 and grew up in the Smokey Mountains of Tennessee. This story is not about him; it is about his father, Ira Ryan. Ira was born in 1850 and was just a boy during the Civil War. I never tell this story without being amazed on how much things have changed in such a short time. Think about it, the fastest way to travel during Ira's days was a horse.

Anyway, this story is about Ira's time fighting during the Civil War when was just a boy. It is 150 years since those days, and you will still be able to hear his voice in this story.

*****

I was eleven when the war of northern aggression started—that is what we in the south called the Civil War. Men from everywhere were leaving their farms and shops to join the Tennessee regiments. Two cousins and the older boys from the farm across the valley were with the first group to go. My pa had a wagon fall on him a few years earlier and walked with a bad limp, so he couldn't go. He stayed home and protected the neighbor's farms.

As I said, I was only eleven. I was too young to join the army, but that didn't stop me. My ma and pa always said that my talk about joining the army was "foolishness." They expected that I would tend the chickens and pigs. I knew I could do more.

On a warm summer night in July of '62, I was three months past my twelfth birthday, almost a man and able to fight. I put a couple of things into a sack, some dried jerky and a couple of potatoes, and quietly departed to join a Tennessee unit. I walked south for two days to Elizabethton. Units were assembling there, men from all over Tennessee and Carolina, some even from Georgia. Many of the men had walked or ridden much farther than me to join the fighting.

I reported to the recruiting building, and the sergeant doing the enlisting just laughed. He said I was too young and too small. I told him that I was stronger than I looked and could shoot through an apple at seventy-five paces, but he just said to go home. I argued, but that only caused two soldiers who were near the door to toss me out of the building.

I landed in the dirt with some force but sprang to my feet ready to show those soldiers what southern men are made of when the local sheriff took me by the shoulder and turned me in the opposite direction.

"You're sure enough brave, but right now, you're too young. Go home, if the war lasts another year, come back. Then, I'll walk in there with you." The sheriff might have been right, but neither that sergeant nor the sheriff was going to keep me from the fighting.

I watched as man after man left the recruiting building as a soldier of the Confederate Army. From there, they assembled on the bank of the Doe River. I heard them talking; they would leave the following morning. So, I finished what was left of my jerky and made my plan. I would just tag along with the men as they left town. Once I was there, they would surely let me stay.

The night was pleasant enough. I found a big oak tree to lean up against and got real comfortable. I probably slept better than most that night. I was up at sunrise and ready to march with the others. Orders were given; there was a short bugle blast, and the men started off. We looked more like a mob than a military unit. A few pretended to march, but most were just walking. The sun was to our backs, so I knew we were going west, but I had no idea where we were going. I didn't care. I was in the army.

No one cared much when I was walking with them out of town; maybe they thought I was just cheering their victory. They acted differently after a few miles. They realized that I intended to go along. Smiles were replaced by shouts and chiding; someone even threw stones at me. "Go on home, kid! Get!" This was going to be a little harder than I thought.

The troop stopped to rest after several hours of marching. The men sat or laid along the side of the road. Some took off their boots, others just relaxed in the soft grass. It was more like a picnic than a war. I was still unwelcome and stayed a stone's throw away from the group. I was glad for the rest. I picked berries as we traveled that morning, so I wasn't hungry. My jerky and potatoes were gone. I needed to find something for later, but I think I was doing better than some of the men lying alongside the road.

The men were up and going before I was ready. I followed them, remaining at a distance. They trudged along throughout the day and by evening met up with a much larger group who had set up camp in a small valley. I don't remember ever seeing that many men in one place in my whole life. Wherever I looked, there were men marching, practicing with bayonets, or reclining near tents. Soon this regiment would be joined to others so that what I was seeing would then seem very small.

I moved away from the group that I arrived with and wandered among the men, staying away from the tents. I didn't want them thinking that I was there to steal. No, sir, it was best for me that I keep my hands and pockets empty. Some of these soldiers had already been in battle. I don't know how I knew it; I just did. They looked tired, and their uniforms were well worn. The soldiers in the camp were much kinder to me that those on the road had been, especially the older ones. It may be that I reminded them of sons that they left back on their farms.

My wandering took me to the cook wagons. The cooks were hard at work preparing meals. It was just dry biscuits and something that looked like soup. It could have been wash water right then, and I would not have cared. The berries I picked earlier were long gone. The cook was a cranky old fellow who possessed a most difficult disposition, but my hunger was bigger than any protests that would come my way.

Spotting me from around the side of the wagon, he pointed a big wooden spoon at me and asked what I was doing. I explained that I had come to fight. I told him of the march from Elizabethton and confessed that all my jerky was gone. "No freeloading here!" he said. "You want to eat? You have to work."

I accepted his offer and did anything and everything that he asked. I washed pots, peeled potatoes, carried water, anything. In return, the cook provided two biscuits and a tin cup of soup. A hungry man will eat just about anything, and I was hungry. I am telling you this because the soup was mostly water with some potatoes thrown in. There might have been some meat in it, but there was none in my cup. My mamma fixes the best biscuits; those were not my mamma's biscuits. Still, they made the hunger go away.

I learned that we were part of the 23rd Tennessee Infantry Regiment. The cook was named Francois, but everyone called him Frenchy. He didn't sound like a foreigner. I imagine his French-sounding name won him his nickname. I always called him Mr. Francois. I introduced myself to him and told him my story. I assured him that I was not going to go back home. I had come to fight.

While Frenchy and I were talking, a captain from the regiment came up to us and asked who I was and why I was there. I told my story again, being as convincing and old as I could be. It made no difference, the captain wanted me out of the camp; he even threatened to have me whipped. I explained that it did not matter; I was going to fight. I could follow the big army just as easily as I followed those men from Elizabethton.

Frenchy offered that since I was so determined that he could use another hand. The captain agreed with a warning, "I don't need a boy under foot, and I will not be responsible for him when the fighting starts. Keep him away from me."

That may not seem very friendly, but it was a lot better than a whipping. Frenchy told me that I could sleep under the cook wagon and would be expected to help prepare the food. I was in the army.

I might start out a cook's assistant, but I would be a soldier before it was over.

That is where it started. I helped Frenchy every day, every day. Frenchy was very protective of the food, so I never did more than carry water, get wood, and clean pots. I didn't want to get Frenchy in trouble, so I stayed in my place.

The regiment engaged in several battles. I saw men who were wounded and some die. That's because it was Frenchy's job to help the doctor. By my thirteenth birthday, I was carrying bandages, helping wounded onto carts, and even worse. I had been promoted to something like a field medic. I didn't have a gun; instead, they gave me a bag of rags and things that I could use to help the wounded on the battlefield. When I left Elizabethton, the men were throwing rocks at me. No one was throwing rocks now.

I am telling you all this so that you will understand what happened at the Battle of Chickamauga. It was September of '63, and the regiment was moving south along the border between Tennessee and Georgia. The regiment was assigned to the corps under General Breckinridge.

Did you know that General Breckinridge ran for president in 1860 against Abraham Lincoln? There were four candidates, and Breckinridge came in second. Sorry, I have wandered away from my story.

Our regiment was dug in just south of Crawfish Springs when the fighting started on the second day. Our Confederate troops would win this battle, but it cost a great deal. I was with a group of men of the far right of the formation. It was bad. We were making our way through muddy, soggy ground. It was hard to move in. Our unit took position in a grove of trees and into some bushes when the fighting started. Shots were fired. The shot was so thick it sounded like a swarm of bees flying overhead; some of those shots were finding targets in our men. I ran from man to man binding up wounds, giving water when I could, then moving to the next. I thought that I heard a man crying on the other side of a berry patch and ran to help him. I didn't find anyone when suddenly a Union soldier rode up on horseback and pointed his gun directly at me. I had no gun, so I picked up a stick to protect myself.

"Who are you, boy?"

I replied, "I'm Ira Ryan from the 23rd Tennessee."

"What are you doing out here?" There was nothing threatening in his question.

"Bandaging these men. I came to fight, and all they did was give me this bag of rags." I wanted him to know that I wasn't afraid of him.

"You're a brave boy." Again, his words were kind.

"Brave man," I corrected.

The Yankee got down off his horse, put his pistol back in its holster, and looked me directly in the eyes. "I believe you are. Now put down that stick."

I put down the stick and didn't know what was going to happen next. I guessed that I was now a prisoner of the Union Army.

"Step closer, boy," was his command. I obeyed the order, taking steps toward the man who was aiming his pistol at me. The pistol might have been in the holster, but he still had a pistol, and I didn't even have my stick.

"Slap me on my cheek, right here." This was the strangest order I had ever been given. It seemed to me that this was why the Confederate Army was going to win the war. Imagine people asking others to slap them.

I followed his order, but I just couldn't hit him too hard; it didn't seem fair.

The soldier then told me this. "Today you have met the enemy, slapped him in the face, and lived. Today, boy, you are a man of valor. Return to your unit. Tell them how you tended the wounded and how when you met the enemy you were unafraid. Take this button from my cuff. This is your proof." He had a tear in his eye; maybe he saw a brother or son when he saw me. Either way, I was alive and free.

I continued to help the men in the field as I made my way back to where we were dug in. When I returned, I told the story to Frenchy, who told it to others.

At the end of the second day, the Confederate Army had won the battle. The regiment was assembled, and we prepared to go to the next battle. The company commander came to me as Frenchy and I were packing up. He had heard Frenchy's story and wanted to know if it was true. I assured him that every word was correct. With that, he sent me home. I was ordered to return home and to protect our farm. A year earlier, I fought to stay, but now I had had enough. I knew I had done my duty, and I knew it was time to go home.

It was late fall when I saw smoke rising from our family's farmhouse. There were no real signs of war here; no one really bothered the mountains much. It looked like Pa had a good year, even without my help. I was hardly in the house when Ma grabbed me and started crying on my shoulder. I don't know what all the fuss was; I had all my parts, not even a scratch.

I stayed at home for the rest of the war. The war had moved far from our little valley, but I could still hear cannon fire and men calling out for help at night. The smell of gun powder and Frenchy's soup seemed to blow in my direction from time to time. I left the war, but it never left me. In time, I heard about the surrender at Appomattox Court House and Mr. Lincoln's promise to help restore the country. I still think about the men of the 23rd Tennessee and that Union soldier I met that day at Crawfish Springs. I'm not sure I will ever forget those things. You know I still have the button that I took off his coat.

* * * * *

Out of the Book and Into the Streets

We hope that boys and girls today will never find themselves in places like those that Ira was in. That does not mean that you cannot demonstrate valor: boldness to speak up for someone, nerve to stand with someone, and the courage to refuse to join the crowd when the crowd is wrong. Earn your own cuff button.

ANTONIO, AFTER 9/11

Do you remember that extraordinary brother whose story I shared? Antonio? Well, I suppose that I need to include another of his stories. I could fill up a day telling stories about him and stories he has told me. This is one that he tells often. It changes a little each time; at the same time, it is always the same. Let me tell you this version and see if you can figure out why he wants to keep telling it.

*****

Antonio has enjoyed a very full, very interesting life. He worked with a United Nations group for nearly ten years after retiring from the air force. Antonio traveled the world with the United Nations. Each host country went out of their way to put their country on display—there were dinners, after-dinner parties, tours, and more. The most memorable of these meetings was the one with the least pomp.

Antonio traveled to Rotterdam, in the Netherlands in the fall of 2001. At this meeting, he joined two hundred delegates from all over the world for a one-week working session. A core group of delegates who attended were at every meeting. Antonio was a member of working group's leadership, so he spent most of his time with this core group. They would dine together and normally be the ones to attend the special events scheduled by the hosting country.

The second week of September in Rotterdam is not the best time to visit. When it was not raining, the sky was gray and gloomy. Antonio has shown me pictures of his visit. Except the picture of a rainbow over the bridge near the harbor, all are a little depressing. Still, the working group meets each year in September, and the

Netherlands volunteered to host the meet, so regardless of weather, they met in Rotterdam.

Antonio's meetings started early on Monday morning. There was the customary breakfast meeting of the leadership and then the stroll to the conference site at the World Trade Center. A cluster of umbrellas moved as a single body along the boulevards, under a cold drizzle. The World Trade Center in Rotterdam was not the giant landmark that I normally think of when someone mentions the World Trade Center. It is tall, but only five or six stories. Like most people, I didn't know there was a World Trade Center in Rotterdam. It turns out that Antonio previously had worked in the World Trade Center buildings in Barcelona, Tokyo, and New York.

The customary greeting time flowed right into the opening sessions for Monday. Antonio and others presented the agenda for the week and invited their host for the week to speak on behalf of the Netherlands. The day was filled with dozens of small meetings, coffee breaks, and more meetings. The group ended the first day on time. Everything that needed to be done that day was complete. It looked like this was going to be a very successful week—no problems.

Tuesday morning started just like Monday, breakfast and then the walk to the World Trade Center. The weather was unchanged; no, it was worse, the drizzle had turned to pouring rain. Everyone was forced undercover if they didn't want to be drenched. Umbrellas were an absolute necessity. Those without scurried from doorway to doorway trying to escape the downpour. In the end, Antonio found his umbrella of little use; he arrived soaked and his shoes squished as he walked down the hallway to his first meeting.

Antonio recalls that he was in leadership meetings the entire morning where the group was packed into a cold, windowless meeting room. There was a break for lunch, and then the meetings started all over again. Working with the United Nations may sound grand, but much of the time is spent in meetings in cramped conference rooms. Antonio was in one of these cramped meeting rooms when cell phones started ringing around the room. Ringing cell phones in one of their meetings is a very serious breach of the rules. Members scrambled to quiet their phones, but the callers were very persistent.

An American delegate finally surrendered and took the call. With shock on her face, she explained to the group that a plane had crashed into the World Trade Center in New York City.

Antonio and many of the others at the meeting had friends in those buildings in New York, so there was immediate concern about the accident. Members left the room to take calls when the meeting host suggested that everyone move into the auditorium where televisions were displaying events in New York. Antonio arrived in the auditorium in time to see a second airplane plow into one of the towers. The entire delegation stood there in shock at what was happening.

The meetings were supposed to continue until five o'clock, but at three o'clock on September 11, all further work group meetings were cancelled. There was only one thing remaining to be done. At the request of our host, and some members from the group, we moved onto the front steps of Rotterdam's World Trade Center. With tears and hugs, Antonio and others offered prayers for the people in the New York and their families. A member of the French delegation prayed for the American people. Asian friends offered sympathies in their own way. As delegates, this group was always formal toward one another. In those moments, they stood with their arms around the shoulders of the Americans, many with tears in their eyes. They pledged their support—anything that was needed, they were prepared to give. These were not just words. These friends were ready to do whatever it took to help.

September 11 events created powerful images. Antonio argues that events of September 12 and the days that followed were more powerful and should be memorialized.

Airports in the United States were all closed following the New York tragedy. No airplanes flew anywhere in the entire country. Antonio was not going home until planes could fly again.

For six days, Antonio was the guest of the Netherlands while he waited for a plane that would return him to the United States. The hotel in Rotterdam found a very nice room for him while he waited to return home. There was nothing to do but wait, so Antonio wandered the streets of Rotterdam and Amsterdam. He took lots of pictures to pass the time—lots of pictures of rainy Amsterdam—but mostly he just wanted to go home.

Some of the delegates left the conference early. One of Antonio's favorite stories about the events around September 11 is about his friend Harry who needed to return home early.

Harry left Amsterdam early on the morning of September 11, flying back to his home just outside of Washington, DC. Harry tells that everything about the flight was normal until suddenly the plane made an unplanned turn back in the direction from which it had just come. The turn went unnoticed by many of the passengers who were busy reading or sleeping. Then the pilot came onto the airplane's speakers and announced that they could not go onto Washington; in fact, they were not allowed to land anywhere in the United States. The pilot assured everyone that things would be fine and that he was awaiting a new destination for the plane.

After a few minutes, the pilot announced that the airplane would land in Reykjavík, Iceland. Harry later found out that flights were diverted away from American airports to sites around the world. Some went to Canada, some were forced to return to where they started, none flew into the United States.

The events in New York were not told to the passengers; to be fair, they may not have been told to the pilots. The pilot announced that the plane would land in Reykjavík with assurances that questions would be answered once the plane was on the ground. Harry remembers the fear that surrounded everyone. Fear went so far as wondering if there was still a Washington to go home to.

The plane landed in Iceland and emptied faster than Harry could remember ever happening before. Everyone was anxious to know why they were in Reykjavík instead of Washington. Television reports were blaring on monitors inside of the terminal. The passengers were getting pieces of information, and all of it was frightening. The important questions had no answers. Important questions like, "How long we will be here?" The only thing for sure was that they were safe on the ground in Iceland, and they were stuck until further notice.

Iceland is a place few would have wanted to be stuck. It would have been worse to be there in January. In September, temperatures ranged from the midfifties during the day to the thirties at night. Harry did not plan for this cooler weather; still it could have been worse. Harry wished that they had been forced to London or Berlin; there were friends and colleagues in those cities. As for being in Iceland, it has only one major city, Reykjavík. It is a pleasant place, but not high on the list of places people want to visit.

Reykjavík was overwhelmed by the flood of travelers arriving on unscheduled airplanes. To their credit, the island country began immediate emergency actions to host their unplanned guests. The city was in the middle of its normal tourist season, so few rooms were available in hotels. What to do? Harry is not sure about other planes that were diverted there, but the passengers on his flight were in two groups. Harry's group became guests in the homes of local Icelanders. When homes ran out, the remaining group was given beds in a local high school gymnasium. Cots and blankets were set up, food and water provided. This was not your regular shelter food. Harry was quick to report that this was good Icelandic stuff. In a home or a gym, they were family to the people of Iceland.

The people of Reykjavík knew as much about what was going on as did their American guests. With limited knowledge, they were prepared to host the Americans for a day or a couple weeks. So, Harry became a long-lost family member who had come for a visit. The same thing happened to others during this time.

Flights resumed after five days, and the Americans started returning home. They were glad to return home and appreciative to the people of Reykjavík. Harry wrote his Icelandic family for years after his visit with them.

Harry wasn't alone. Other of Antonio's colleagues ended up in Canada, some in Quebec and others Montreal. Their stories are not as spectacular as Harry's, but Canadian compassion was just as real.

Antonio holds that something good, something global happened following the tragedy in New York. It didn't matter where you spent those few days before getting back to the United States. After being stranded in Rotterdam for a week, Antonio finally got a flight home. Something was different on that flight. The flight from Amsterdam to Washington normally took seven hours. International travelers, especially business travelers, surrender to the challenge of being locked inside an airplane for a long flight home. Before the destruction of New York's World Trade Center, people boarded the airplane, said their required "hello," and then settled in for the long flight. Families talked among themselves, business travelers spoke very little. Many travelers spoke not a single word during the entire flight. Antonio's flight was different. People talked. It was real talk. They shared their stories of the past week—why were they in the Netherlands and what had they done to fill their time. They talked about families; wallets were out sharing pictures of children and grandchildren. They talked about their jobs, but that seemed less important. There was a kindness that extended to everyone on the plane. The flight attendants were not airline employees; they were fellow travelers—they had been stranded travelers just like everyone else.

It was dark when Antonio's plane landed in Washington. Despite that, every passenger on the right side of the plane strained to look out the windows as the plane neared Washington; perhaps they could grab a glimpse of the damaged Pentagon. The plane landed, and everyone clapped and cheered. They were home.

The newfound kindness of people did not end when Antonio left the plane. It went beyond the airport. It continued for a long time after September 11. People talked on airplanes and while standing in line at the store. People formerly ignored were suddenly seen and extended kindness. As a country, we boiled with rage at those who had destroyed the towers. We also experienced a renewed sense of community. We were unified and kinder.

Time went on, and people began to forget. Airplanes were packed with people who returned to their silence, quietly moving from place to place. Stores were filled with shoppers who are willing to fight over a sale price item or complain about a long wait in line. And the homeless, well the homeless once again turned invisible. We returned to life as it was before September 11.

Antonio's story goes on. He points out that the spirit of September 12 has returned again and again. But sadly, he will say, "Too often it takes a national or personal disaster to awaken that spirit."

TALES OF THE STORY KEEPER

Antonio recently told me that he had seen the spirit of September 12 alive again following a terrible hurricane the tore the little island of Puerto Rico apart. Power was lost across the entire island, not just for fifteen minutes but for weeks. No power meant no water—no way to cook, no way to bathe. There was no air-conditioning, not even a fan to move air around during those hot humid nights. It was terrible, but somehow in all this, the very best of the Puerto Rican people was drawn out. Before the storm, everyone was busy with work and their families. People were not unfriendly, just distracted by work, school, after-school soccer, and a hundred other things. After the hurricane, the lights went out, and there was no place to go, and there was no gasoline for cars even if one wanted to go somewhere. Neighbors discovered one another. Families gathered together under a community lamp—they looked after one another. It was common for families to share a community meal. They brought what they had and made a communal meal. Children played together, and adults sat and talked. Families would sit together and play board games. Of course, the lights came back on, and things slowly returned to normal. But for a while, the spirit of September 12 covered the island of Puerto Rico.

Antonio is sure that there are similar stories about hurricanes that pounded the coast of Texas and Florida. Antonio's question is, "Can there be a general change in the way our modern, high-speed world behaves without homes being blown away?" He looked for instances of widespread September 12 behavior in the hi-tech world that he lives in where there was no September 11 event preceding them. So far, he hasn't found one. Every occurrence of September 12 behavior has an associated September 11 event. Still, Antonio keeps telling me that he is sure that it does not have to be that way.

* * * * *

Out the Book and Into the Street

Most who are reading Antonio's story were born after September 11, 2001. It is an event in a history book or a news report as the anniversary of the day arrives. It has become something like the Alamo and Pearl Harbor. It was very real to those who lived it, but not so much now. So was September 12 and the days that followed. Antonio is still looking for signs of September 12. He still believes they are few and far between. We hope that he is wrong. The kindness of September 12 did not happen when a law passed or a committee met. It was individuals deciding to extend kindness. Can you find a way to extend undeserved kindness to someone in your community? Maybe we should propose that September 12 become the National Day of Kindness.

CHARLIE, CAMPING ALONE FOR THE FIRST TIME

Uncle Jeb, you might remember that some call him Biscuit (I could never do that), well, he has three children, a boy and two girls. We might have a story about my cousin Emma, but it is JD's son that I want to tell you about now. I'm sorry, I should have told you that JD was short for Jeb Daniel. Jeb was named after his father. When he was very small, they started calling him JD—I don't think that I have ever called him anything else. Anyway, JD married and moved out to Idaho with his wife. He worked for the forest service. The couple had a son, and sometime later, JD lost his wife in a car accident. JD and his son, Charlie, continue to live there in Idaho.

I sat with Charlie at a reunion of my mother's family last year. Charlie told me this story, and now I will share it with you.

* * * * *

It was early October in southern Idaho. The colors in the trees are amazing at that time of year. Already the paths in the forest were covered with an even layer of brittle leaves that crackle when you step on them. According to the sun, it should have been about eight o'clock. The slight chill in the air made it a perfect day for Tink and me to be out. By then, we had been hiking for about an hour. Hiking is too strong a word for our progress, just wandering better describes our pace. My dad's advice helped slow our pace. He always said, "Be more content with having a good time than making good time." My dad would have been proud of the precision with which we executed his words.

At that time, I was thirteen. I have spent my entire life in those woods. I came home from the hospital to the house we live in. I have never known another home. My parents built the home a couple of years before I was born. They purchased land adjoining Niagara Springs State Park where my dad works. They built their dream house on that land, and if I have anything to say about it, it will be where I live my whole life.

Tink, well, Tink is my dog. Or just maybe, I am Tink's boy. Tink was my birthday present the year I turned six. My mom met a rancher in town who was trying to rid himself of a litter of puppies. She just couldn't resist taking the runt of the litter home for me. Tink's official name was Tinker Bell. My mom thought the tiny dog needed a tiny name. Well, it did not take long for Tink to outgrow that name. No one knew what she was; I always say she is part lamb and part lion. Tink tips the scales at seventy-five pounds; she is big. She is even bigger thanks to a thick coat of long white fur dotted with splotches of gray and brown. When Tink plants her paws on the ground, curls up her lip, and begins that low growl, she becomes a real force to deal with. Still, I'll tell you that Tink is a whole lot more lamb than lion.

On that day, Tink was just wandering in the woods with me. Sometimes she was at my side; other times, she was exploring sounds coming from off the path. Regardless, I was never out of her sight. I never worried. That's what Tink always does; besides, I had taken this hike dozens of times with my dad. If I kept the sun shining on my left shoulder, I would reach the campsite. My dad set up a small place near the bank of the Snake River where the two of us go from time to time. Boy how I love being outdoors and how I love being with my dad.

This trip to our fishing camp was the first time for me to spend the night alone. It had taken a lot of pleading with Dad, but knowing that Tink was going along, Dad agreed to let me spend one night. I was loaded with everything I needed to be warm and fend off hunger before departing. I planned to have fish for dinner, but just in case, there was something in the backpack for both me and Tink.

My mind wandered, thinking about the fish, thinking about setting up camp, and looking forward to building a fire. Suddenly, my attention was called back to the path. Leaves were rustling off to the right of the path. It wasn't Tink; she was exploring up ahead. I stopped, and the rustling stopped. I wasn't scared. If it was anything to worry about, Tink would have known. It might be a small squirrel or chipmunk. It could have even been an echo from all the noise I was making as I shuffled along the path. Did you ever notice how much fun it is to kick up the leaves on the path?

Satisfied that there is nothing there, I resumed my walk. Now, Tink never lets me get too far out of her sight. Maybe she heard something too or maybe she just wanted to be close to her boy. Either way, Tink was now walking step-for-step beside me. I had not gone more than fifty yards when the rustling started again. Tink still was not alerted to anything, which seemed curious, so I decided to ignore it and continue our hike to the campsite.

I walked, and leaves rustled. I kept checking off to my right, but I couldn't see a single leaf move. Tink started to wander ahead again—there is no way she would leave me if there was something out there—so I became sure that I was hearing the echo of my footsteps.

I came out of the woods into a small clearing not far from the river, a little later than planned. I had spent too much time looking for ghosts or something during the hike. I was maybe a quarter mile from where I knew I should be. The only thing to do was to follow the river to the campsite. The lean-to that my father constructed on one of our earlier trips was still there, waiting for me to take my place. Even the firewood was there. We piled up logs before leaving the last time so there would be plenty of firewood for our next visit.

I had done this before. I knew the first order of business was to get the fire going. Kindling littered the ground, so within no time, the firepit was ablaze. With the fire going, I stowed the rest of my stuff and took off for the river—fresh fish was preferred to canned meat.

What a day for fishing! The sun was bright, the sky was clear, and there was almost no breeze. This time of year, the breeze can make things uncomfortable on the river, but on this day, I enjoyed fishing until all remaining daylight was gone. I stood right there on the bank of the river coaxing my dinner to come to me.

Tink normally was content to wander the bank for a while then find a place to lay in the sun. She wanted to wade in the water and chase leaves falling from the trees. It was fun to watch her, but it was no help at all as I tried to lure fish onto my hook.

I was surprised to hear the rustling start again along the edge of the trees. I knew it was not me this time, and I still saw nothing. Maybe Tink was too busy chasing leaves to hear what was going on. This had gone far enough; I was going to find where that noise was coming from. Just then, dinner grabbed my lure. The rustling leaves would have to wait.

The fish hit the lure hard, and from the feel of it, I was going to have work for supper. The fish darted toward the bank and quickly back out. I had been here before. Judging from the tug on the line, this was one of my favorite fish—rainbow trout. Judging from the fight that the fish was putting up, Tink and I just might have leftovers.

The battle did not last long. It wasn't even a fair fight. I only had to take my time and let the fish tire out once the hook set deep into the fish's jaw. A few minutes of tugging and thrashing ended with a prize trout being carried back to the campsite.

I forgot all about the noises coming from the edge of the forest. Why? Because I was too busy cleaning that great big, beautiful trout, all the while promising Tink that she would get her share. My dad would have been proud of how skillfully I cleaned that fish, just like he taught me. The fish was ready for the fire, but it was too early to eat, so I wrapped it up and put it aside. The fish would still taste fresh even if it was an hour before it was skewered and spinning over the fire.

With the fish ready for cooking, I started thinking about those strange noises from the woods. It was time for Tink and I to going looking around and finding whatever was causing the mysterious noises. There is a truth about being in the forest, or in my case, at the edge of the forest. When you are alone, it's best to go exploring when there is daylight. Too many things can happen in the dark. Dad told me more than once, "You are a lot more likely to hurt yourself than have something hurt you when wandering in the dark." I wasn't afraid that something was going to hurt me. Tink was all the protection I needed. Warning or no warning, I was sure that something was causing all those noises, and I was going to find out what it was.

The noise was coming from somewhere along the path, so I decided to start searching back where the path ended. The two of us returned to where the path opened out onto our clearing and started a very careful hunt for what had been invisible all day.

The walk back to the path revealed nothing—not one sound out of the ordinary. Tink wasn't sure what she was looking for, but since I asked her along, she was going to hunt. Her steps were slow; after all, she had been very comfortable lying in the sun. As we got nearer to the entrance of the woods, she began to perk up. One of Tink's' top five things to do was stroll in the woods. The others are related to food, sleeping, food, playing, and food.

Tink and I made our way into the woods following the path we were on earlier. Nothing. Something caught Tink's interest, but it was just some old scat, probably left from a fox or raccoon. I stood dead still for a long while, but the only sound I heard was Tink's breathing. Neither Tink nor I were having much fun, and a fish was waiting to be cooked, so we called off the search and returned to the campfire.

I turned to start back when once again the leaves on the ground made a little rustling sound. I ran to where I thought the sound was coming from. I made so much noise that there was no way to know if there was someone or something else there. It didn't matter, there was nothing there. Tink had started running when I sprang out after the noise, but Tink just thought I wanted to play.

It was useless to keep this up. Tink would have been all over whatever was running around out there if there was something out there. That didn't happen. She just sat by me wondering what to do next. The sun was starting to go down and a fish was waiting on us, so the only thing to do was to return to the campsite. With that, we set our steps toward our waiting dinner.

The fire had burned down some, but the logs were still ablaze, and the coal bed was ready to cook the trout. I pushed a stick down into the fish and propped it over the coals with rocks that were there just for that purpose. I packed cheese and crackers in my backpack just in case the fish were not biting. Since they did bite, I decided that Tink and I would munch on the cheese while the fish cooked. Tink looked at me like this was one of the best ideas I had all day. I sliced some cheese off the block, one for Tink and one for me, and together we sat by the fire watching the sun go down, enjoying our appetizer. This was exactly the way things were supposed to be.

Unless you have eaten fresh trout cooked over a campfire flame, you cannot possibly know how much I was looking forward to dinner. Tink and I nibbled on little pieces of cheese, but when the main course was ready, the real meal began. I removed the stick from our dinner and carefully carved it, removing the bones for Tink. She does a good job of grinding them up, but I would rather make sure she doesn't get poked by her dinner. Two portions were placed onto pieces of tin foil that I had brought along in my backpack—fine dinnerware for this special dinner. I added crackers to each plate and put Tink's plate down for her.

Together we sat eating and watching the last rays of the sun. I can tell you that I savored every bite of that trout, placing small bits of fish on the crackers. Tink was less graceful. She devoured everything except the tin foil. I guess I am a real softy when it comes to Tink. I didn't mind tossing a bite of food to her when her plate was empty; it was bits of crackers first. It was harder to part with the trout, but even some of that was tossed her way.

Cleanup was simple. The stick used to cook and the wrapper from the crackers was tossed into the fire. The tinfoil was folded and returned to my backpack. Done.

I added a couple of logs to the fire and began settling down for the evening. Tink and I would have no trouble sleeping tonight. All the walking and fresh air make sleeping easy. I hoped to do some exploring in the forest the next day as we made our way home, so I didn't plan to stay up too much longer.

The last couple of logs that I added to the fire must have been green because the fire was puffing out clouds of white smoke. The smoke turned into shapes that I assigned to animals and bugs from the forest. It was relaxing. Tink was no help with the game. Her belly was full. The warmth of the fire and the events of the day were enough to cause sleep to come to her.

As I looked through the smoke to the other side of the campfire, I saw the silhouette of a small person sitting cross-legged on the ground. Now I know you think that I am crazy, but I strained to make out what he was seeing, certain that there was something there. I had seen rabbits and squirrels in the sky, but this looked like a person—not floating in the sky but sitting across from me. All that time Tink didn't make a sound, never paid a moment's attention to the form that was now visible to me.

I remember asking, "Tink, do you see what I see?" I needed a little help, a witness to the impossible. Tink just laid there, full of fish and crackers, enjoying the warmth of the fire.

I couldn't help it. I asked, "Hey, are you real?" If there was someone there, I was going to find out. I was more than a little scared now, especially since Tink seemed to be no help at the time.

The wisp of a person seemed to look at me and respond, but the sound was too faint to make out. My visitor continued to speak, and slowly the voice became loud enough for me to understand the words—still no response from Tink.

I think I must have been the bravest boy ever or the stupidest. I was talking to a smoke figure.

"Who are you? Do you have a name?" If there was someone there, I was sure as shooting going to find out.

The figure's response was weak, too weak for me to make out. My visitor was just an outline of a figure. I decided that I needed a name for whoever or whatever I was seeing, so I decided to call it Casper. To be polite, I introduced Tink and myself. I could have just as well ignored Tink's introduction. She was still warm and full. She didn't even twitch when I said her name. My guest, Casper, didn't budge from his place by the fire.

Bewildered is the only word that could explain how I was feeling at that moment. Maybe I should have been afraid, but no alarms were going off in my head. I knew that I wasn't dreaming. I was fully awake—Tink was the one that had sailed off to sleep. So, I just sat there not knowing what to think. I just sat there seeing what would happen.

Casper sat there not seeming aware that I was sitting directly across from him. His attention was captured somewhere in the fire. Every few moments he looked in my direction, but then his eyes returned to small flares that rose up out of the fire. I was certain that if there was going to be a conversation, I was going to be the one to start it. Truthfully, there was something of a conversation occurring, at least it looked that way. Casper hadn't said anything that I could hear, but he appeared to be talking to someone. His lips moved, but not a sound was heard.

I peppered him with questions. "Well, Casper, what are we going to do here? Is there something I can get you?" That kind of stuff. The fish was gone, but I still had a little cheese, and Tink didn't eat all the crackers. This seemed as good a place to start a conversation as any.

Casper again looked to be speaking, but nothing came out. As Casper continued to talk and gesture, I began to hear the faint sound of a voice. I leaned forward and closed my eyes trying to put every sound away except the faint voice that I thought was coming from Casper. Slowly the voice became clearer. It was the voice of a young boy not much different from me. He was talking about being in the forest and something about not needing anyone else.

Aha! It was Casper that had been following Tink and me all day. He was the source of all the leaf rustling that I heard along the path. That still did not explain why Tink did not hear him.

As I sat there, the voice became more and more clear. Casper told me that he had seen me earlier in the day and wanted to know why I was way out here by myself.

I was glad to know that I wasn't crazy but still surprised that Tink didn't notice Casper. I know that anyone who hears my story may think that I am a little goofy, but I promise you that Casper was there.

I wanted to answer Casper with the same questions he put to me, but that is rude. I explained that my dad and I normally come here together. I told him that we had been there many times and that we were the ones who built the lean-to that was behind me. And I told him that I just wanted to have some time to myself. Of course, I wasn't alone; I had Tink.

Casper wanted to know why my mother had agreed to let me go alone. He seemed to think that mothers don't approve of boys hiking in the woods.

I explained that my mother died in a car crash about six years ago and that it was just Dad, Tink, and me now. It was easy to correct him about my mother. She loved the forest. If she were still here, she would be proud of me staying out here. I probably said more than I should have, but my mom loved this forest as much as I did. I was positive that she would have packed my lunch and kissed my cheek before I left the house.

I pressed Casper again to learn his story. Why couldn't I see him except through the smoke? It was his turn to provide some answers. He just said that he didn't know what my problem was. He said that he could see me just fine. Then Casper just started asking more questions about the woods and more questions about me. Did I have bothers? Wouldn't I rather be camping with a friend? On and on with questions.

It was no secret that I was an only child. If my mother had lived, I might have had a younger brother. Things didn't work out that way. Our house is miles from town, and the closest neighbor is a mile away as the crow flies, and the closest boy near my age is nearly five miles. I insisted that I was alone, and I liked it that way. Then I pressed again to know his story.

Casper explained that he did not choose to be as he was. He wanted to play and do the normal thing that other kids did, but everyone just ignored him. He almost cried when he talked about wanting to be picked to play on a team or to be invited to birthday parties. The end of his story ended with a simple, "They just don't seem to see me."

This was all sinking in. I didn't know what to say or how to make Casper feel better. I told him he should feel good knowing that I could see and hear him. He then told me that it wouldn't last for long. When the fire died down or the sun came up, he would be lost. Then questions started again. What about you? What do you like? What is your school like? Do you play sports? It was clear that Casper needed to talk.

Casper's questions sounded more like a thirsty man begging for water. Strangely, I seemed as anxious to tell my story as Casper was to hear it. I started talking about Dad and his work in the forest. I moved through life at home and continued onto school. I talked and talked. Casper focused full attention on me, not missing a single word.

The fire was starting to die down, and the night chill was beginning to gnaw at my hands. I threw a couple more logs onto the fire, and the flames were soon leaping again into the air. More smoke billowing from the logs, and Casper's form remained seated. Except for some occasional swaying, Casper did not move one inch the entire evening.

It was getting late, and I was beginning to feel the drain of the day. I wanted to spend more time with Casper, but my eyes were getting heavy. He wanted to keep going, but sleep was going to win out. I didn't know what Casper was going to do, but I had no choice. Sleep was pulling at me too hard.

I finally surrendered to my sleeping bag's call. I told Casper good night, crawled inside the bag, and with a pull of the zipper, I was out. Tink took her cue and curled up at my side. With fire on one side and Tink on the other, I slept well that night.

I sprung out of the sleeping bag at first light. Tink was already up, exploring on the edge of the river. The morning air was crisp, and I was sure that I needed to get the fire going again before anything else happened. I tossed a few small pieces of kindling into the fire pit and poked at the coals until the flames awakened. I then added larger pieces, and like a true woodsman, I had a blazing fire belching out heat and smoke.

It was then that I remembered Casper. I squatted down beside the fire and squinted to see Casper through the smoke. He was not there. Nothing. There was not a single sign that Casper had ever been there.

Tink started barking down by the river. I was sure that Tink had finally seen Casper, but I was wrong. Tink was excited about a family of raccoons that were out for a morning walk. Momma raccoons can be ugly when they are protecting their babies, so I called Tink back. Tink's fun was spoiled, but she obeyed the call. She was at my side, but Casper was gone.

A beautiful morning, wandering raccoons, a river full of fish, but no Casper. I wasn't sure why, but things were just not right. Any other time I would have been scampering off to tease trout with my favorite lure. This morning, I was just thinking about going home—straight home. Any other morning, I would look forward to prowling through the forest, tracking deer or finding berries; today I was thinking about home.

It didn't take long to break camp. Things were packed up, and river water had drenched the fire. The fire, I couldn't leave the fire. My father would never approve of me leaving until I was sure the fire was completely out. So, I waited and hoped maybe to catch a glimpse of Casper through the last wisp of smoke. Casper was as gone as he had been all morning of the day before.

With my backpack slung over my shoulder and Tink as my side, I started for home. A slight morning breeze blew across my cheek and caused an occasional stir of dry leaves on the floor of the forest. More than once, I stopped to see if Casper was following. After an hour of starting and stopping, I gave up hope of seeing Casper again.

The last half of the march home was in total silence. Tink was her normal self. She would be at my side one moment and then dash off the path in response to a squirrel that was just trying to find some additional nuts for the coming winter. I was glad that Tink was tromping around; at least, I could be sure that the noises I was hearing were real.

I was nearing the trailhead when I noticed a small group of boys coming into the woods. I had seen these boys before at school. Their faces were familiar, but I didn't know them, and I suspected that they didn't know me. Anyway, the group was about fifty yards off to my left. Tink noticed the boys but was far too busy chasing squirrels to be bothered by them. They seemed to look in my direction, so I greeted them with a wave. They did not see me. I gave a second, weaker wave, but still no response. I wasn't surprised. We went to the same school and never talked. I sat in my place, and they sat in their place.

I was home before noon. The house was empty; my dad had been called back to help with something in the forest. I just brushed Tink down and then settled into playing video games and some television. I couldn't help looking around the room wondering if Casper might have followed me home, but I was alone.

* * * * *

Out the Book and Into the Street

Charlie and I talked for a while about his time in the woods. I began to wonder, who was really the invisible one? Charlie couldn't see Casper. The boys couldn't see Charlie. I also began to wonder about other people who might be invisible, people whom others overlook all the time. I wondered how we can help them become visible. Look today to help someone who might feel invisible to you. See the person who is sitting alone. See the person who is always picked last or always walks home alone. Start with just one person.

JEB DANIEL, CHASING WILD BOAR

Uncle Jeb's son Jeb Daniel is an interesting fellow. I mentioned him before; he is Charlie's dad. Remember? Jeb Daniel is his given name, but I have called him JD forever. He is a ranger in a state park out in Idaho. It's no surprise, he has always loved being outdoors. One of my favorite stories from JD is about time he spent in Florida. I like telling this story, especially after JD has just finished telling the family about chasing a rogue bear or some other backwoods adventure. But I'll stop and let him tell it firsthand.

* * * * *

The summer after I graduated from high school, I decided to drive down to Florida and spend a few weeks with friends of the family. My old pickup truck wasn't pretty, but it was dependable, so the drive was uneventful.

Florida was nothing like Pennsylvania. It was flat. It was also humid. Breezes off the ocean at night helped some, but it was still hot.

The family that I stayed with had a house that was inland from the Atlantic Ocean in south Florida. It was still close enough to the coast that I could feel the breeze at night. I could drive from their house to the beach in less than an hour, which is exactly what I did, every day, for the first week or so that I was there.

The Martin family used to live in Pennsylvania, just down the street from our house. Our families were close before the Martins moved away. They decided to move south at the end of my junior year of high school. Bob, their son, and I were buds since grade school. I really missed him after they left. Besides Bob, there were two younger girls—Marie who was a year younger than Bob and Trisha who was two years younger than Marie. I don't remember missing them.

I arrived at Martin family's house just in time to say good-bye to Bob who suddenly joined the army and was leaving for boot camp. It was a disappointment, but I determined to make the best of it. The offer to stay at the Martin house was still good, so I had a place to crash.

As I said, I spent the first week at the beach. The Martin girls were always up for some time at the beach, so I had plenty of company. The problem is that I am not an ocean kind of guy. I can swim, but sand can never replace soft grass. The open sky is beautiful, but I need trees. That is why after the first week of surf and sand, I started looking for other things to do.

I planned for Bob and me to do some camping while I was there, my camping gear in the back of the truck. With Bob not around, I decided that I would just enjoy a little camp outing by myself. Funny, the girls were always quick to volunteer to go with me to the beach, but there was not a whisper from them when I talked about camping.

Camping in Florida is different from camping in Pennsylvania; like I said, it is flat. Also, the ground is mostly covered with low brush and palmetto bushes. There are pencil-thin pine trees and a few live oak trees—mostly thick brush and palmetto bushes. There is also lots of water. Small ponds and canals crisscrossed backcountry. I want to be clear. I was not going into the Everglades; my camping site was more civilized than the swamps of the Everglades.

I planned to spend the weekend. I would camp, fish, and hike if that was possible. It would have been great if Bob were going along, but somehow this trip started to take on an air of personal freedom. I was a high school graduate out on my own.

I should tell you that wildlife in southern Florida is different from wildlife in Pennsylvania. We don't have alligators in Pennsylvania. I saw them in the canals but never met one face-to-face. They also have panthers; I never met one of those either. They have bears and pigs; we have those in Pennsylvania. It is the pigs that are important to this story.

Florida is home to a large population of wild hogs. These are big, mean hogs. They can weigh two hundred pounds. Did I say they were mean? The story is that their ancestors were brought to Florida by the Conquistadors in the 1600s. Some hogs broke free from their pens and wandered off into the Florida brush where they married and multiplied. I was smart enough to know that you should give them space, at least I thought that I was.

Anyway, I like to think of my adventure more like running with the bulls in Pamplona. Do you know about that? This festival dates all the way back to the fourteenth century in Spain. I know that Papa Rafa will tell this story saying that the tradition goes back to Italy but really started in Spain

* * * * *

Hold on right there, JD! I normally do not interrupt a storyteller, but I would never make such a mistake. Italy gave the world beautiful art, music, government. Michelangelo, Raphael, Da Vinci, Pavarotti, Bocelli, Vivaldi, I can go on and on. But Italy would never boast about such a crazy thing as running with bulls. No, we are people of culture and beauty, not men with the seats of their pants gored through by an angry bovine. Never.

* * * * *

Forgive me, Papa Rafa, but you do give a lot of credit to Italy. So, I'll continue.

People have gathered for years to run with the bulls in Pamplona. I once tried to learn what started this whole thing. In the beginning, the bulls were just driven through town on the way to market. The streets were narrow, so early in the morning, the people would stay in their houses, and the herds would be rushed through Pamplona. I suspect that there was a young Spaniard boy who wanted to impress his favorite Spaniard girl. The starstruck Spaniard probably trotted ahead of the bulls, screaming out her name to prove his devotion to her. Before it was over, he was just running and screaming.

Today, the streets are still narrow. Only, now hundreds of people line up for the privilege of outrunning a bunch of angry bulls. When I was younger, I wanted to go there to be part of the festival. I have lost that urge.

What does that have to do with the boars of Florida? I'll tell you.

I traveled about twenty miles from the Martin's house and found a dirt road that led into the Florida wilderness. I followed the dirt road until it turned into a path that followed a canal. I drove down that path until I came to a clearing, not far from the canal. There, I set up camp.

Late on the morning of the second day, I decided to take the truck further down the path to a small pond that I discovered the evening before. I hoped that the fishing there would be better than in the canal—so far, I had nothing to show for all the time my hook had been in the water.

I was approaching the pond when out in front of the truck I spotted three piglets. These were very young wild boars. I estimated that they weighed less than twenty pounds, closer to ten.

I had been in the woods many times. I knew that unless something had happened to the mother of these piglets, she was close by. It didn't take long to discover where she was. The mother was about thirty yards, maybe a little more, from the babies. She was foraging for food among a clump of palmetto bushes. She seemed to be completely unconcerned about my being there as she was rooting in the ground around the bushes.

At that moment, an idea came to me that might have been best ignored. The Martin family had a few farm animals on their property. There were two horses, a couple sheep, and a pig. It seemed to me that adding a little pig to their animal collection would be a nice way to say thank you to them for letting me stay at their house.

How to do it? That was a question for which I quickly constructed an answer. I backed the truck up as close to the piglets as was possible. The little guys were wandering here and there, so I had to be happy with the spot I found. I was able to get within maybe ten yards of the piglets, and momma pig never gave me the first look.

I had a plan worthy of a high school graduate. I had a fishing net in the back of the truck—it was a net strung on a large hoop at the end of an eight-foot pole. I planned to creep up on the piglet, net one, and then run to the truck. I was young and fast, and momma pig was too distracted by whatever she found on the ground under that palmetto bush. This was an excellent plan.

The piglets made things difficult because they kept moving from place to place. One moment they were close, the next moment they doubled the space between them and the truck. The real problem was that I didn't have all day. Momma pig was not going to leave those babies forever. In the meantime, I sat in the bed of the truck, fishing net in hand, waiting for my chance.

Soon the little guys came wandering back toward where I was parked. I wasn't going to be picky. The closest pig was going into the net. These pigs weren't going to hurt anyone; they were just babies. So, I climbed down out of the truck and carefully moved closer and closer. Finally, I stood as straight and still as one of those pine trees; my chance was coming.

I had the net over the little pig in one swift movement. Then I twisted the loop to secure the little guy, and as fast as I could, I raced for the truck.

All the piglets started squealing. The one in the net was making the most noise. Momma pig responded more swiftly than I had expected. I had no idea that hogs could run that fast. I took one step, and she took four. I ran, the piglet squealed, the other babies scattered, and momma kept coming. Worse than hearing the approaching pig feet was the chomping. Momma was slamming her jaws together with every other step. The pop of those teeth coming together showed clearly that she intended to get her baby back and make whoever tried to take the baby pay a price.

The piglet was not helping me at all. My mistake was not considering how difficult it would be to carry the pig at the end of the pole. I had the pole to the fishing net thrown over my shoulder so that maybe six feet of the pole extended out behind me. The pole would bounce as I ran. I wouldn't be surprised that the little pig thought the ride was fun as he flopped up and down. But he got heavier with each step I took.

I was less than five feet from the truck when it was clear that I would not reach the truck before momma pig reached me. I did the only thing I could do. I dropped the fishing net and dove into the back on the truck, just ahead of the nasty teeth of momma pig.

Even then I was not sure that I was safe. The wild hog stood up on the back of the truck, making ugly sounds and continuing to slam those jaws together. I climbed onto the top of the truck and waited. She went around and around the truck, butting the tires, trying to stand up on the running boards, she was not going to let me just leave without a spanking, pig-style.

In the meantime, the little pig worked free of the net and had wandered to join the other piglets. I imagined him telling the story of his ride in the net, bragging about his mother, and then all of them laughing at the boy on top of the truck.

It didn't take too long for the piglets to wander back into the palmetto bushes. Momma was not going to let them get too far from her sight, so she gave up her rant against me.

I waited for a long while before I decided to test the waters. Finally, I was sure that the coast was clear. That did not keep me from leaping as quickly as I could into the cab of the truck. I didn't want to lose that fishing net, but I wasn't going to walk back and get it. The only safe thing I could do was back the truck up, open the door, grab the net, and then quickly close the door again. This worked exactly as planned, much better than the last plan that I had.

Well, I returned to my campsite, happy to catch fish from the canal and happy that I didn't have a big hole chewed into the back of my pants. I never saw those pigs, or any others, during the rest of my camping time.

I did not mention the pigs to the Martins when I got back to their house. I was sure that they would call my parents with the story, and it would only make them worry about me. This was my first time away from home after high school, and I didn't want them to think that I wasn't responsible enough to be out on my own—it really doesn't seem like I was when I think about what bad judgment I used.

So, there you have it. I never went to Pamplona to run with the bulls, but I did go to Florida to run with the boars. And you know what? Neither of those is really a good idea.

*****

Out of the Book and Into the Street

JD's experience with the wild boars tells us a lot about how instinctively parents are designed to protect their children. Your mother is certainly tamer than the momma pig, but be sure she would be just as committed to protecting you. Take a few moments and thank the adults who are watching over you. How about, "Thanks for keeping me out of the net." They might not get it. Maybe it will start a conversation.

JEREMY, THE SNAKE

I haven't told you anything about my younger brother Jeremy. He is the free spirit of the family and the source of dozens of fun stories. The last time I counted, he has lived on five continents, in eleven countries. He tagged baby seals in the artic and followed orcas in the Pacific Ocean. I have recorded stories about the sands of North Africa and the kangaroos of Australia. There are so many stories to choose from, but this story about working in Thailand is often requested by the family. I will do my best to tell it with the same energy that he normally does. I promise you will want him to tell it when you see him—just to see the expressions on his face. Listen now as Jeremy tells his story.

* * * * *

  I had no idea what I wanted to do when I graduated high school. I knew that I didn't want to go to college—I wanted to see the world, to dig my toes into the warm sand of the beaches of the Mediterranean or stand on the mountains of Tibet. None of that was going to happen in college. Therefore, my plan was to fill my backpack and head off to far-off ports. I had read a lot about tramp steamers, ships that moved from port to port without a real schedule, so I hoped to work my way across the ocean and then move on from there. A job announcement in the Sunday morning paper changed all that. There on the classified page was a large ad looking for someone interested in working in Asia for a communications company. It was a job for unskilled labor. No experience needed, one-year contract, and they were going to pay me. I applied for the job before the day was over and departed for Thailand in less than three weeks.

That job started twenty-five years of wandering from one adventure to another.

I flew to California, then to Hong Kong, and finally arrived in Bangkok. There I met the team that I worked with for the next eighteen months. Yes, I know. The newspaper ad said one year, but there was more work to do, and I stayed until it was done.

If I could have made up my job, it would have looked exactly like the one that I found in Thailand. I worked fourteen days straight, but then I was off for five whole days. I took advantage of the long breaks to travel around the country. Three times I visited the northwest corner of Thailand. I walked through apple orchards that belonged to the king of Thailand. I rode elephants in the teak forest. I went to the southern beaches a half dozen times. Those beaches were a favorite vacation spot for Europeans. I made friends on the beach at Maya Bay on Koh Phi Ley that I was able to visit later when I was working in Norway. But you don't care about that; you want to hear about that time in the jungle when I was up on the Laos border.

My job was to help set up communications towers around the country. Most of the towers were in the middle of nowhere. One of the first worksites that I was assigned to was in the northeast corner of Thailand, not far from the Mekong River. We were there for almost two months. Normally, it took half that time, but we had to clear the jungle that kept growing back. The weather was no help either. It was midsummer and monsoon season. It seldom stopped raining, and when the rain stopped, it was unbearably hot and humid. We worked in the mud and rain most of the time we were up there. Between the rain and the sweat, my feet were never dry.

The rain was a problem. Critters were another. Most critters were harmless, but the smaller they were, the more they could get on your nerves. Small flies and mosquitos were everywhere—my bed was covered with a net so that I could sleep. There were a few small monkeys. I only saw them from a distance. For sure, frogs and lizards made up the largest group of critters. They were everywhere. Frogs would be stuck on the side of our tents and the trees. There was no place that lizards didn't show up. They would sometimes startle you by falling from a branch or crawling out of your boot, but like most other things in the area, they were harmless.

There were also snakes. Jungles and snakes just go together. The problem is that some of those snakes were nasty. As bad as some were, they all would leave you alone if you just left them alone. Twice I met a banded krait, twice it was at night. The banded krait is very poisonous and best left alone. Neither encounter with the snake was initiated by me. Once the snake was crawling across the floor next to my bed, and the other time it crawled across the ledge by the windows of our room. Both times we agreed to go our separate ways, and all was well. In addition to the banded krait, there were also cobras, and not just one kind. I was told that the bite of a cobra can kill an elephant, so I made it a point to stay as far away from them as possible. Just to be clear, I stayed far away from all snakes as possible—I don't like snakes.

The worksite where we were building the tower was a long hike from where we lived. A single-lane road, more like a wide, muddy path, connected the two places. We used a rusty old pickup truck to move between the two. For those times that we felt adventurous, we had a bicycle that we could ride, but the ruts and mud in the road made it tough to ride the road, especially at night.

Many times, I just walked the road. Early morning and nights with a full moon were the best time for walking. Walking required caution, but it was safe. I walked right down the middle of the road. The idea was to avoid the crawly things that frequently lived just off the side of the road. I carried a flashlight that helped protect me from anything that might be on the road. If I paid attention, I was perfectly safe and so was the wildlife.

The tower was nearly built, and I was anxious to be done. Workdays were long, and to be honest, we took some shortcuts that we normally would not have taken—we were tired of the mud and the rain. Taking shortcuts can cause you problems.

The team was wrapping up for the day, and I decided to stay so I could finish stacking pipes so we could begin shipping stuff down south. That was the first shortcut.

I finished the job just as it was getting dark. I had a radio that I was supposed to use to call someone to come get me, but it would take them longer to get the truck and get me than it would for me to walk back to the campsite, so I decided to walk. That was the second shortcut. It might not seem like a shortcut, but that night, there was no moon, and it was very dark. I had walked that road dozens of times, so it didn't seem like a bad idea, and I had my flashlight.

There was no magic to walking down that road. Just do your best to get as little mud as possible on your boots. There were lots of ruts in the road to be avoided. There was lots of mud to tromp through. There were also lots of critter noises. Bugs and frogs sing loudest at night, and that night was no exception. You would not think that a little beetle could make much noise. They make quite a ruckus when there are a million of them. That night, there was something else.

The moonless sky made the stars come alive. There is just no way to explain how big the night sky is in the jungle. Most of the time, there is a canopy of trees that covers you, but the road between the worksite and the campsite was clear overhead. There was nothing between me and the farthest star. The edge of the Milky Way was unmistakably visible on that moonless, crystal-clear night.

I used my standard walking technique as I started down the road. My flashlight scanned left, then scanned right, then scanned ahead of me. Following my other walking rule, I stayed in the middle of the road. The problem that night was the sky. I was maybe halfway down the road when I was captured by the beauty of the sky. It was impossible to ignore. My flashlight continued its normal sweep. It went left. It went right. It shined up ahead. But I started paying more and more attention to the stars. I picked out constellations that I knew and was amazed at how much there was up there that I had never seen before. That is when it happened.

I remember seeing a muddy rut in the road and instinctively I stepped over it. Then I remember feeling something under my left boot. Yes, under my left boot. This is something that I will never forget. It did not feel right, so I came to a complete stop and shined the light down at my feet. There under my foot was the head of a snake, a cobra. I was sure that it was a cobra. I had seen several cobras since arriving in Thailand, but never like this. I shined my flashlight to find that my right foot was firmly planted further down the body of the snake. This was not good.

I remember this like it was just yesterday. My mind began to race, thinking about the right thing to do. What do you do? I never once imagined that I would meet a cobra, face-to-face, or as it was face-to-foot. I received no training for "what to do when you step on a cobra." I clearly remember being told to just leave the snakes alone. Going back to high school, I don't remember even one hour dedicated to that subject. I needed a plan. No, I needed a good plan.

It didn't take that long to come up with a plan. I decided I had no choice. The only option was to run, but how? Cobras are very fast. This one might be even faster since I had made him angry by standing on his head. My plan was simple. I would make sure that I started my retreat with my right foot. I needed to keep the biting end of that snake away as long as possible. Next, after I stepped off with my right foot, I would step down hard with my left foot—pushing the snakes head down in the mud seemed like a good thing to do. Finally, I would keep running, as fast as I could, until I got away or the snake got me. It wasn't a fancy plan, but it was the best I could come up with at the time. By the way, it did occur to me at that time that I wouldn't need a plan to run away from a cobra if I had gone to college instead of Thailand.

One, two, three…I took off. I ran like I never run before. I never looked back once. I just kept running. I ran until the road ended, and I was inside the campsite. I ran into the mess tent where we ate and slammed the door. I didn't know where that snake was, but I hoped it was back on the road somewhere wondering what had happened to it.

My buddies were just finishing their dinner when I came flying in the door. I don't know what they thought when they saw me. I looked a mess. I stood there, out of breath with mud all over my boots. I started to explain about the snake when one of them told me that he had seen that same cobra when he was returning from the worksite. He had whacked it hard with a machete and was pretty sure that it was dead. I was standing there in shock, and they were uncontrollably laughing at my expense.

Dead? That possibility never came into my mind while I was standing there on the road. Dead? I had run like crazy down that muddy road to get away from a dead cobra—something else could have gotten me while I was racing away from a dead snake. Dead? No, I was certain that if I raised my left foot that I was the one that would be dead.

So, there you have it, my encounter with a deadly, dead snake. Since those days in the jungle, I have traveled around the world. I've worked in some very strange places, and I am glad to report that the one time that I thought I was in real danger, the danger was a dead snake.

* * * * *

Out the Book and Into the Street

There are a lot of reasons that I like to tell this story. I like to consider that Jeremy's shortcuts caused the problem. If he had paid attention to the walk, he might have known that the cobra was not a problem. I like to consider Jeremy's description of the night sky. How often do we have a chance to stare into the universe, but we keep our eyes on the ground? I like to consider the reality of Jeremy's situation. How often are we afraid of something that represents no harm to us? The challenge here is to find your follow-up action. Are there shortcuts that you are taking that are making your work less than it could be? Name them and get rid of them. Are you too busy to see the big picture? Spend some time gazing into the night sky. Is there something of which you are afraid but really can't hurt you. Face the fear. Ride the roller coaster or the Ferris wheel. Try out for the baseball team or concert band. Be fearless, do the right thing, and don't miss the bigger thing.

JOSEPHINE, TALKING WITH HENRIETTA

As the story keeper, I capture stories from the family and share them whenever the opportunity arises. I keep the stories exactly as they are told. The accuracy of the story's facts is the responsibility of the one who tells the story to me. Honestly, sometimes I wonder if the fish was as large as they boast, but it is not my job to judge. This story from my sister Josephine is a perfect example of a story where the facts may not be exactly right. I am sure that my eyebrows raised, and my face betrayed my doubt as she told it during dinner one evening. The problem is that Josephine is just eccentric enough for it to be true. See if you agree.

* * * * *

As you all know, Henrietta Bobowitz is my cat. She's about ten years old now. She's becoming a little cranky with age, but she is still a great friend. I suppose that you find her name a bit strange. I must tell you how she got it. It comes from a book I read when I was a young girl. I so liked that book so much when I read it back then that I gave the main character's name to my cat. I've read it again now that I am older, and it doesn't seem as funny, but back then, I rolled around on my bed squealing with laughter—my mother more than once demanded that I calm down. But as a girl, I saw every crazy thing that the 266-pound chicken did and loved all of it. The chicken was named Henrietta, and she lived with the Bobowitz family.

Now that you know where the cat's name came from, let me tell you about Henrietta Bobowitz. My Henrietta was a strange-looking creature as a tiny kitten. Her fur was sort of yellow with splotches of white. The fur didn't lay down; no, it stood straight up—all over. She looked like a little troll doll, or as I saw her, a little chick. I remembered Arthur Bobowitz's chicken. So, there you have it. My little kitten became Henrietta Bobowitz, named after a gigantic chicken. Though I never called her that, it's too long, but it is her name, nonetheless.

Henrietta is no regular cat. She is more human than I can explain. It's probably my fault. She has a nice little cat bed that stays in the corner of my bedroom, but she sleeps in the bed with me every night. She has a very nice food bowl in the kitchen, but she eats most meals sitting on a chair next to me. Many evenings when I am having tea before bed, I will put Henrietta's milk into a teacup and let her lap the milk from the chair next to mine. And there is more, so see, you can't blame her if she thinks that she is more than your standard house cat. Now that you know all of that, let me tell you the most remarkable thing about Henrietta.

It started about five years ago. My week had been terrible—no, it was worse than terrible. I'd worked long days for weeks to get a project done at work. When it was almost done, the project was canceled. All my work was for nothing. Added to that, I started getting a cold a few days before. I couldn't breathe out of my nose, and I was hurting all over. I was in no mood for company. I locked my doors, turned off most of the lights, and turned on some soft music. I was just going to ignore everyone and everything. I would relax, away from all thoughts of work and my stupid cold.

I sat down in the overstuffed chair in my den and began sipping a hot cup of peppermint tea, which of course I sweetened with a full spoon of honey. Henrietta was sitting in her normal spot lapping warm milk from one of my special teacups. Things were so pleasant. The aroma of the peppermint reached deep inside of me, and for the first time all day, I could breathe out of my nose. I might have even started to doze off when I was startled back into the room, fully awake.

"Why do you keep doing this?"

What! The voice had broken into my perfect evening jolting me fully awake. I jumped from my chair and fixed my attention on the hallway leading to the front door. If I had had X-ray vision, I would have seen into the house across the street—that's how hard I was staring. Nothing. There was no one to be seen. I tell you the truth, I was somewhat frightened. My heart began to race. Someone was at my house, and I didn't know who.

I shouted, "Who's there?" I really didn't want a response. None came. I offered the question a second time, more timidly than the first, but the only sound I heard was the soft music from the radio playing in the background. That was it; it must have been something on the radio. With that thought, I started to regain my calm. I had just started to sit back down in my chair and…

"Why do you keep doing this?"

I was too far down to stop my sitting, I just flopped into the chair. I grabbed the chair's arms and leaned over to look around the floor. I was sure that the voice had come from the room. It was not a big voice, not the husky voice that I imagined would belong to a burglar. It was very clear and matter of fact. It was more like the voice of a friend trying to help another friend through a difficult time.

"Okay, show yourself!" I was in no mood for games, and I was still very anxious. I was sure that I was alone. "Who's there, and what do you want?"

"I don't really want anything, thank you."

That time I knew where the voice came from, or at least I thought I knew where the voice came from. I shook my head. I pinched myself. I looked around the room for other answers. When there was no other explanation, I said, "Henrietta, did you say something?" I focused my full attention on that cat sure that the reply to my question had to come from somewhere else.

"Yes, I did. I've held my peace around here for far too long. So tell me, why do you keep doing this?"

For the moment, I thought that I might be losing my mind. I tried to blame my cold; maybe I was sicker than I thought I was. I tried to blame the glass of wine that I had earlier with dinner, but it was only one glass and a small glass at that. I tried everything to explain what was happening, but I had seen Henrietta's mouth move, and I heard the words come directly from her. I remembered something from a philosophy class I once took. It went something like, "The more assumptions you have to make, the more unlikely an explanation." If that were true, then I had to accept that I was talking to my cat.

"Henrietta, you have been with me for years. Why are you just now talking?"

"Well, to be honest, I just didn't have anything to say."

I suppose that was as good an answer as any. Still, it didn't seem to be the answer that I needed right then. That cat had lived in my house, eaten at my table, and slept in my bed. Was she able to talk all that time and remained silent? Did she really understand when I talked to her? Oh, some of the things that I said when she was little—it would've been better if she had not understood some of those. I needed more. I especially needed to understand why Henrietta chose this time to disclose her little secret.

"All right, you have my attention. Now, what was it you wanted to say?"

Henrietta once again offered the same question, "Why do you keep doing this?"

"Doing what?" I didn't really understand what she was asking. It had to be something besides our having tea in the den.

There was a slight purr in Henriette's voice. She had transformed from my pet into my therapist. I wouldn't have been surprised to see her put on a pair of black, horn-rimmed glasses and take out a pad of paper. There were no glasses or pads of paper, but she did continue. "You are clearly not happy with what you are doing. You come home every night, growling about the day you had. You don't think I know, but I have seen it all. So, why do you keep doing it?"

I didn't know what to say. I mean, I was explaining to a cat. Who does that? Well, maybe a more correct question is who does that and expects an answer? The bigger truth was that I didn't know the answer. I invented the best response I could and said, "Well, we need to make the house payments somehow."

Henrietta the cat was suddenly Henrietta the sage. "Why do we need to make house payments?"

It took only a second to reply, "We need someplace to live." Can you believe that I was having this discussion with my cat?

"Henrietta the Wise" went through a series of questions each one starting with the word "why." I was becoming frustrated with her digging deeper and deeper into my life when she asked the final question, "Why do you have to live?"

I couldn't form an answer to that question that wasn't more than just "because." It was then that Henrietta helped me understand what I really needed to do.

"I am a mouser," Henrietta said. "Everyone expects me to catch mice. They also assume that I will kill the little rodents. They would be wrong. I was born to be a mouser, but my passion does not include the murder of those little guys. There is nothing that I enjoy more than a good chase. When I tire of the chase, I catch them, but they will live to be chased again. Oh, I smack the little guys around like a hockey puck. The game is over when they are too dizzy to get up."

"You mean that my house is full of mice?" That thought had never come to me before.

"Not full," replied Henrietta. "There are a few, but trust me, they would much rather forage for food outside than journey into the kitchen. Even the bravest ends up wobbling back into his hiding place. And do you know why? Because I love to be a gentle mouser. It is what I was born to be."

"But we aren't talking about mice. We are talking about you." Henrietta left the role of a cat and resumed her counselor's tone. "Why are you here? What is it that you were born to do? What do you really love to do?"

I knew the answer the moment the question was asked. Pottery. The teacups Henrietta and I drank out of, I made. Most of my free time was spent reading about, planning, or making pottery. I played with the idea of having a small shop where I made and sold pottery but was too scared to take the chance. Henrietta was right. I needed a change, and the change should be something that I enjoyed doing. I could do many things. I needed to do the thing that was right for me.

"Henrietta, you are right. I need to do something else." I was sure she was right.

Henrietta accepted my agreement with her just as she did almost everything else. She turned, flipped her tail a few times, and walked away. The conversation was over. She did not say another word the entire evening. Oh, I tried to engage her. I asked questions, offered cat treats, made silly little noises to attract her. Nothing. She just laid on the couch. Her eyes were half open as she gently purred.

I wrestled with myself that night. Did the conversation really happen? Did I really want to open a pottery shop? What would I tell my boss? Voices played the questions inside my head all night. There were other voices. The voices that told me that I was crazy, that I had a good job and should not leave it for a dream. There was even a voice that told me that I wasn't that good at making pottery. If I couldn't make pottery, how was I going to make enough money to live? What a night I had.

The next morning, I went into the office and quit. When my boss asked why I was quitting. I told him that my cat had suggested it. That seemed to make it easier for him to accept.

I leased a place for my pottery shop a week later. I still work and sell out of that little shop. I named that shop "Purrfect Piece." Maybe each piece is not perfect, but I have a lot more peace than when I was working in that office.

I make beautiful pottery. Cups, saucers, bowls, pitchers, the list goes on. If you look at the bottom of anything made in the shop, you will see the image of a dizzy mouse. That is my way of thanking Henrietta for helping me get started.

As for Henrietta, she speaks from time to time, only when she has something important to say—at least important to her. I never know when. I have become only slightly accustomed to that little voice. It still startles me. Our last conversation was about barking from the new neighbor's dog. It seems that the puppy barks when left outside too long and can even howl when he wants to go inside. It's a puppy, and I am sure he will learn as he grows older, but Henrietta proposed that she be the one to teach the dog some new tricks. I think she thought that the puppy was just an oversized mouse. Anyway, she has moved past that for now. We continue to enjoy sitting together in the evening, me with my tea and her with her milk, served in

Purrfect Piece teacups. And be sure, I am always listening just in case Henrietta has something else to say.

* * * * *

Out the Book and Into the Street

    Maybe Henrietta can talk, only Josephine and Henrietta really know for sure. Still, the advice that came to Josephine was good. Do what need to be done but seek things which you really love. Boys want to be astronauts or firefighters. Little girls might want the same thing. Focus on whatever that thing is. Maybe it will change over time. Astronauts become pilots; firefighters become doctors. Start now by asking, "What do I really like?" or "What am I really good at?" Then, chase after those things.

SILAS, THE DIVING TEAM

You may have noticed that my stories come from all age groups. It doesn't matter how old my family members are, most have a story to tell. This story is from my sister Josey's oldest son, Silas. By the way, the family knows him by the nickname of Skeet. Silas is one of my favorite nephews. He was always moving when he was small. He would swing through the branches of the trees, launching himself into the air and onto the ground. He would climb up on the roof and walk along the ridge—much to my sister's dismay. It would not have surprised me to see him walking the high wire or flying from a trapeze in the circus. He was full of energy. Anyway, Skeet is in college now studying somewhere in New Mexico to be a geologist. His story comes from his high school years. It is guaranteed to whet your appetite for more of his stories.

* * * * *

I can't remember a time when I didn't love the water. I don't remember taking swimming lessons, but I remember being in the swim club when I was six. I wasn't a diver then. I was swimming freestyle and butterfly events against boys my age. I'm no *Aquaman*, but I was good enough to compete. I collected a drawer full of second and third place ribbons during those first few years in the club. There were some silver and bronze medals—only a few gold. It's no surprise I turned my attention to diving by the time I was nine. Maybe it was because when I was diving, I was competing more against myself than against swimmers in the other lanes, maybe because I won more often. It could also be that I enjoyed the feeling of spinning in the air.

Eventually, I was diving from the ten-meter platform, over thirty feet above the water, but like all divers, I started on the springboard, three feet above the water. It is the springboard that is at the center of my story.

I remember learning to dive from the board. Three feet looks a long way down when you are only four feet tall. It took some coaxing from my dad to get that first dive. Even then, I didn't dive. I just jumped in, feet first. I sank down, popped up, and knew that I wanted to do it again. After several jumps, I tried my first dive. I remember my dad coaching me. He said, "Don't think too much, Skeet. Just lean over and touch the water. Let gravity do the work." I slowly bent over the end of the board—hands together, arms straight, head between my arm. An inch at a time, I reached toward the water. When you lean over, there is a point of no return. It's that moment that you know you can't stand back up. You have two choices. You continue to reach for the water, that would be a dive, or you try to stand back up, and that would be the world-famous "belly flop." I've done more than one belly flop and a few back flops since that first day, but on that day, my hands and feet stayed together, and I entered cleanly in the water. That started my love of diving.

My junior high school did not have a swim team, so I developed as a diver and competed with a local swim club. I earned a place on the high school swim team my first year there, so I left the swim club. I earned a school letter all three years for swimming. It was my only sport.

Our high school swim team was above average. We won some swim meets; some of our swimmers were very fast, two girls competed at the state level. Three boys were divers. We didn't compete in any other event. The team's best diver was a guy named Barton Alexander; everyone called him Arrow. Arrow was a junior. He was tall, very strong, and known across the state for his tight spins when he jumped. Arrow was okay. Sometimes he could be full of himself, but he was the best of the divers, so it was overlooked. My other teammate was Tim Ulrich. We took turns being in second place behind Arrow. Regardless of who was the better—and it was always Arrow—we were the boy's diving team. We had been diving together since we were young. We were friends, and we supported one another—in the pool, around the school, everywhere.

Swim teams are a lot like cross-country and track teams. The largest group of fans in the stands are parents and girlfriends. In my case, there was no girlfriend until my senior year. The cheerleaders and marching band never showed up, and you only found a concession stand to get a hot dog at state meets. We just showed up, swam, and went home.

Added to the general popularity of the sport was our mascot. We were the "Bears." It's hard to imagine a bear powering down the swim lane in a freestyle race or doing a back double somersault in the pike position. We cheered for one another, "Go Bears!" I seemed to lack something. Honestly, none of the school mascots fit the image of a swimmer.

There is not much to say about my sophomore year. I was the youngest diver and not a serious threat to the older divers in our conference. Tim was in the same boat that I was, so Arrow had to carry the load for the diving team. He competed against seniors and stayed right with them dive for dive.

Practice my junior year started exactly where it left off the year before. I, on the other hand, was different. I was bigger and a little stronger. I guess I grew into my body over the summer. It didn't matter; building strength and diving basics were still the focus. I don't know how many times I heard, "If you don't get the basics right, nothing else matters." Each dive was broken down into its elements, and then, I worked to perfect each element. Nothing fancy, just perfect. It was during the first week of practice that disaster stuck.

Arrow was up on the springboard preparing for a routine dive—an inward dive in the pike position. He stood on the board with his back to the water. He was supposed to spring from the board, turn toward the board, and enter the water without a splash. He'd done that dive thousands of times, but something happened. When he leaped up off the board, he leaned into the dive too early. The back of his head caught the edge of the board, and he tumbled down into the water like a duck shot out of the air. There was the awful slapping sound of a dive gone wrong and then blood from the gash in his scape began to color the water. Without a moment's pause, the swim team was in the water helping Arrow out of the pool. Cuts to the head bleed terribly; they appear worse than they are. Arrow's rock-hard head suffered no real damage. There was only a small cut. It only took a few stitches to hold his head together. It was hidden under his thick blonde hair, so he didn't even get any sympathy from the girls. But smacking the platform had hurt something that stitches didn't fix.

Arrow returned to diving two weeks after his accident. Any remnant of his injury was neatly hidden under his dark-brown swim cap. Our old diving partner was back, but something was different.

The coach didn't change practice just because Arrow was back. He was marching toward the pool area with his whistle in his mouth and clipboard in his hand when he started his routine, "If you don't get the basics right, nothing else matters, and, Alexander, no more blood in my pool." He wasn't as heartless as he sounded. That was just his way of saying, "Be careful." On the other hand, his words promised a very hard practice. Dive after dive we focused on the basics. It was boring and safe. Arrow worked through the practice, but his dives were flat. They were best described as "safe." Our best diver was only average.

Practices continued for days, but the school's best diver wasn't improving. Something was knocked out of him when he hit his head on the board. He looked the same, but his dives were safe. The dives were technically correct, but they lacked the beauty, and some of the daring, that had been so easy for Arrow before the accident.

It seemed clear to me that our team wasn't going to win many competitions this season unless we could find the old Arrow. The worse part was that the entire team's timing seemed to be off. The racers were slow getting off the blocks and were having trouble in their turns. The basics just weren't right. It wasn't Arrow's fault, but somehow, it all seemed to have started after Arrow's accident.

I was telling my dad about how things were going and how we were going to get crushed this year. Dad said to me, "Skeet, you guys are overthinking this. You are so focused on execution that you are missing the bigger picture. Your muscles know what to do if you will just let them. Think back to your first days on the platform. You jumped in feet first, you fell in headfirst, and the next thing you were flipped and twirling. Relax and have fun. See what happens."

It sounded too easy, but Dad had been right so many times before that he just might be right this time. I decided to make a game of diving, and I hoped I could draw Arrow and Tim into the game whether they knew it or not. I tried to think of what I was going to do while Tim was beginning his warm-up. Suddenly I was given the key to the game. Arrow had teased Sydney out onto the board. Now, Sydney could dive but didn't like it very much—she wasn't afraid, she just didn't like it. Sydney's presence on the board invoked the diver's golden rule, "the only way down from the board is into the water." So, Sydney grabbed her nose and spun off the board, feet first, into the water. A picture flashed into my mind that had nothing to do with the girl falling into the water. She would've never talked to me again if she thought that the image in my head had anything to do with her.

Inside my head was projected the picture of a giant hippopotamus wearing a bathing suit, carrying an umbrella. It was something from a cartoon I saw when I was younger. My vision of the umbrella-carrying hippo, along with my dad's advice to "relax and have fun," changed everything.

I wasn't sure exactly how I was going to get Arrow and Tim to go along with the game, but I knew that I had to start it. Tim hadn't climbed onto the board yet, so I just stepped up and said, "I think Sydney's got something there. Look at me, I am a diving bear." With that, I leaped off the board and produced the most dreadful splash a diver could make. It was a half-cannonball and half-belly flop. The first rule of diving is that you should enter clean into the water. *No splash* was one of the basics. I had just reached the side of the pool when Tim crashed into the water, sending a huge wave over my head. Bear number two was in the pool.

Tim and I badgered Arrow to join bear clan, but he would have no part of it. He was a senior and the captain of the squad. It was hard for him to join our underclassman game. My second leap started like a practiced dive but ended in a cannonball of the highest caliber—

water went everywhere. I popped out of the water and challenged the other two to try and beat my last dive. I stared directly at Arrow with a smug, half-smile that was no less than a direct challenge.

I had just pulled up out of the water when a tidal wave covered me. It took a few seconds before I could clear the water from my eyes. To my surprise, it was Arrow in the pool, not Tim, and there were whitecaps all over the pool. I wish I could have seen that dive; it must have been a doozy. Arrow shouted as he made his way to the side, "So, Skeet, you ready to give up?"

"No way! We're just getting started."

I changed the rules when I got back on the board. Bears don't fly; apparently, they can't dive either, so we needed to be something else. This time, it was penguins. Penguins can't fly, but they do a darn good job of entering the water.

"I'm a penguin. Watch this!" I performed the most basic platform dive, focusing on entering as cleanly as possible. I clamped my arms to my side, locked my legs together, and cut into the pool like a knife. The only record of my dive was the bubbles I left behind. "Beat that!" was the challenge I issued to the other two. Tim was first and then Arrow sliced into the water.

There was only so much of our clowning around that the coach was going to allow, so we settled back into our practice routine. It was not our best practice but was the most fun that the three of us had had in a while. It certainly was not going to be enough to turn us into a team that could win against schools in our division, and we were only a couple weeks from the first swim meet.

I have seen the perfect dive in my mind, felt gravity pull on me as I twisted and fell toward the water, and heard the swoosh of the water as I entered perfectly. I had never really done it, but it would someday be my dive number six. The part of that dive that always captured me was soaring. It didn't last long, but it was beautiful. That was the next round of our game. I determined I would lead Arrow and Tim in a soaring contest.

We were getting ready to start our practice when I asked Tim, "Have you ever seen one of those animal shows where flying squirrels leap from tree to tree?"

"Sure, who hasn't."

"Well today, I am going to soar like one of those squirrels." I said that knowing that soaring from the springboard is about the most fun you can have. I stepped to the edge with my back to the pool and only my toes remaining on the diving board. Then I got a good bounce and fell slowly toward the water with my arms outstretched, my back assumed its arched position exactly as the muscles had been taught, and my feet were glued together. My entry into the water was near perfect—that was what soaring looked like. Soon after Arrow and Tim were soaring into the pool.

It seemed that we were in more of a hurry to get back onto the board. It was Tim who took the lead. His entry could have been better, but the soaring part made up for the entry. Arrow smiled at me and took his turn. I followed. Things were getting back to normal.

Arrow, Tim, and I played our game at almost every practice, and for some reason, the coach never complained. We didn't play the whole practice, but we did manage to make our way through the animal kingdom during the days leading up to our first swim meet. More and more attention was spent on things that fly. I remember trying to be a dragonfly. That didn't work very well.

The day of the first swim meet came, and we thought we were ready. It was a dual meet where our team was swimming against just one other school. They weren't our biggest worry for the season, but they were good. The meet was set up in the normal three parts, two swimming event sections and the diving. The dive team competes in the middle of the meet.

Our swimmers had done well; now we had to do our part. Divers would attempt six dives. There are five general categories. Each diver would perform one dive from each of the five categories, and then a sixth dive was something chosen by the diver. The sixth dive could come from any of the five categories—it is the diver's special dive.

As the visiting team, we dove first. A Bear would dive, and then one of the other team would have their turn. One of us and one of them for six rounds.

Tim was the first Bear to dive. His dive was not his best, and the score was low. I was the second from our team on the platform.

My dive was less impressive than Tim's dive. There was not enough height to finish the dive the way it should have been done. I knew it wasn't pretty, and I didn't even see it. Arrow was last into the water. I thought that he was technically perfect and was sure it would score high. Still, he would need more if he was going to win this competition—his dive was too safe.

We were standing silently behind the springboard waiting for our next turn, licking our wounds. We were off to a slow start, and we knew it. I turned to the other Bears and said, "Hey, guys, I don't know about you, but I feel like a little flying. This bear is going to use his wings. I'm not going to win today, but I am going to have some fun." It was good that we kept that little conversation to ourselves. The coach would have given me what for if he had heard me accept defeat after just one dive. Still, I just said what all of us were thinking. Tim gave me a big grin and started toward the end of the board.

There was great height in Tim's second dive, height that was not there the first time on the board. It would score much better than that first dive. The other team's diver missed his entry. His feet slapped the water. His mistake would help us, but we were going to need more help than that to win. It was likely that the first set of dives had cost us the meet. It was then that we agreed, the best we could do was enjoy ourselves. The Bears became the falcons and swans and eagles that day.

I watched as Tim and Arrow flew from the end of the board. We didn't pay any attention to scorekeeping; fun was the order of the day. We kept encouraging the eagles to fly higher and swans to land softer. It was the most fun we ever had at a swim meet. We were louder and crazier with each round.

It was the sixth round, and Arrow was standing on the board. The rounds had flown by, and our last diver was preparing for his last and most difficult dive. The entire swim team was there cheering our best diver. Arrow looked back, and Tim was flapped his arms like a seagull or maybe a chicken; it was hard to tell. Why not? There was nothing to lose. Arrow used all the power the board could generate to launch him above the water. He reached the peak of his dive, turned back toward the board, twisted, and then entered the water.

He ripped into the water with that *swoosh* sound. It was so clean that not a single drop of water dared to make a splash. It was a dive worthy of our best diver. What am I saying? It was a dive worthy of anyone's best diver.

With that, the divers retired from the competition. We found seats next to the pool and cheered for the swimmers during the second half of their swimming. We were just glad that we were done. We couldn't undo the mistakes of that first round. We did our best, and now it was time to help our swimmers. Tim was not shy about shouting when Sydney was in the pool. Sydney had held her nose when she jumped off the diving board a few weeks back. She wasn't holding her nose that day. She churned through the water like a machine. She won the butterfly and backstroke events. No one was even close to her when she finished the butterfly event. Overall, our team did very well.

The overall scores for the diving competition were announced last. Third place did not go to a Bear. No, the award went to one of the best divers in the division, a senior who was unaccustomed to being in third place. Arrow was announced as the second-place finisher. I didn't pay any attention to the other divers that day, so I can't be sure that Arrow might have deserved first place, but considering his nasty fall only a few weeks earlier, I was happy for him. Then they announced Silas Taylor had won first place. I just stood there with my teammates cheering for Silas when I realize that I was Silas Taylor—I'm so used to being called Skeet that I guess I just forgot. I have no idea how that happened, but I know that Dad was right. We had some fun and let our training work for us.

The dual meet was over. The overall scores were very close, but the combined score of the Bears was not enough to beat the other team—we blamed the first round of dives. We would have been happier to have won the meet, but we had a lot to be happy about. Arrow won second place and didn't whack his head, I somehow managed a first-place win, and Sydney sat on the bus next to Tim on the way back to the school. Everyone had something to be glad about. And we had fun.

We had nine more meets that season. I was never the first-place diver again that season. Arrow returned to his old form and returned to first place over and over. He graduated at the end of that year, and Tim became captain of the diving team. As for me, I did no competitive diving after high school. I turned my attention to teaching. Along with my teaching chores, I coach diving for the school's swim team. The good news is that the school's mascot is a bumblebee. At least it flies.

* * * * *

Out the Book and Into the Street

Friends sometimes need encouragement. We don't encourage them just to win the prize; we encourage them because they are our friends. Today would be the perfect day to help a friend. Take a moment and think about your friends. Is there someone you can encourage?

SARA, THE BALLOONING ADVENTURE

My younger sister, Sara, is the most down-to-earth member of my family. Sara was the oldest girl, but far from being the oldest child, so she was well protected by the older brothers. Maybe it was our fault, but she grew into a woman who liked things to be predictable and safe. Never the explorer. Never the risk-taker.

Sara graduated high school, attended a local community college, and finished her teaching degree less than ten miles from where she grew up. Our family was stunned when she accepted a teaching position in southern Indiana. A year after Sara started teaching, the family was flabbergasted when Sara announced she was going to marry a man that she met in Indiana—her fiancé wasn't even Italian! We're still not sure what he is. He thinks that Olive Garden serves Italian food. Momma leaves the room whenever he says that.

I must let Sara, the one who never takes a risk, tell you her story of a less than normal school day. I can still hear her giggle whenever I think about her encounter with the hot-air balloon. It just might make you giggle a little too.

*****

I wasn't sure what I was going to do when I grew up. I was sure that I would never move away from my family. After finishing my student teaching, I received a call from a former professor who had moved to Indiana to work for a local school district. She offered me a job teaching in one of their elementary schools. The school was described as a small-town school, one of the older elementary schools in the district, where almost all the fourth-grade teachers retired at the end of the last school year. I'll never know why, but without a second thought, I accepted the offer. It is more than twenty years since that phone call, and I am still teaching at the same school.

New Albany, Indiana, is exactly as I was told years ago. It is a small town just across the river from Louisville, Kentucky. We enjoy the small-town life and access to big-town activities. Most of the parents of my students make plywood in the local factory. Some of these parents were my students years ago.

Our town enjoys a series of small-town festivals throughout the year. I have come to enjoy those which happen in the fall most of all. In addition to our Founder's Day, Mule Day, and Fourth of July celebrations, we also receive the overflow from some of the big-town events occurring in Louisville. The biggest of those that spill into our community is the Kentucky Derby. The Kentucky Derby is more than an event. The people of Louisville spend an entire month on derby things. Most of them stay on the Kentucky side of the Ohio River, but occasionally, we are included. My story takes place during the weeks before the Kentucky Derby.

Louisville hosts a hot-air balloon festival every year. The festival takes place a couple of weeks before the big race and draws dozens of hot-air balloons from around the country. It is great fun to attend the evening balloon glow. In the dark, the balloonists light their burners and inflate the balloons. The burners light up the inside of the balloons so that they become giant night lights. They keep the balloons tethered to the ground; they don't fly, only ascend about fifty feet. It is beautiful. Hanging in the sky, there are constellations of colorful luminaries.

It was 2008. I was nearing the end of another school year, derby month started in Louisville, and the annual balloon festival was nearing. Our school received word that three balloons from the festival were going to come to the school and present a short flight demonstration for our students. We were told that the balloons would arrive on trucks early in the morning. The pilots would prepare the balloon for flight in the field in front of the school and then rise to about thirty feet while tied to the ground. There was more. Each balloon would take to the air, although only a short distance off the ground, with a teacher on board.

Our principal turned the balloon demonstration into a citywide event to raise money for the school. All the teachers were entered into a contest to see who would ride the balloon. Parents and students, all willing to part with fifty cents, were challenged to buy votes for their favorite teacher—just fifty cents a vote. The money raised would buy new books for the school's library. The three teachers receiving the most votes would earn a place in the balloon's gondola and wave at the students from on high.

The physical education teacher received the most votes. He was a well-liked, young man who also coached a local basketball team. I wasn't surprised when his name was announced. My surprise came when the name of the second teacher was announced. It was me! I never imagined I would win. I never wanted to win. I wasn't sure I wanted to accept after I won.

To be honest, I didn't know what to do. I didn't want to go up in the air. I was sure they didn't have seat belts in those baskets. At the same time, I didn't want to disappoint all those who spent their lunch money so that I could ride. I couldn't let the other teachers think that I was afraid. I didn't, I didn't, I didn't. The only "I didn't" that mattered was, I didn't want to go!

I worked up the courage to accept my fate when the principal delivered yet more good news. The local papers and a Louisville television station would have people reporting about the balloon event. With that, I started feeling a little sick. I resigned to go up, but I planned to close my eyes as soon as the balloon started up and keep them closed until I was sure we were firmly on the ground. I wasn't sure that I could summon a smile and a wave that I would want to see in the newspaper. How was I going to do that with cameras clicking all around me? I started praying for rain or high winds, anything that would keep the balloons on the ground.

News reporting which teachers were going to take the balloon rides spread quickly. Excited students from past years and parents from the present were sending me notes and leaving messages. The well-wishers were under the impression that I was eager to take the balloon ride. I didn't have the heart to tell them that I would rather have a root canal without Novocain. I had become known for having a sharp tongue in class when the situation required it. I said things like, "Suck it up, buttercup," periodically to lazy students. Now, "suck it up, buttercup," seemed to be the only way I was going to get through this balloon thing.

The morning arrived when I was to ascend in a little basket under a big balloon tied to the ground. I dressed for the occasion. I thought it might be a little cool, so I wore a gaudy sweater that had a big horse on the front, black slacks, and tennis shoes. The hot-air balloons were in town because of the Kentucky Derby, so I thought the sweater with the horse was a nice touch. I brought along a ball cap, but I didn't plan to wear it since I knew it would mess up my hair. The other teachers were also dressed for the occasion. Of course, the gym teacher was wearing a jogging suit. He had pulled a T-shirt over his outer jacket that had New Albany's high school bulldog printed on the front.

I suppose we were as ready as we were going to be. The principal was flitting around; she appeared more nervous than I felt. She reminded each of her airborne teacher corps that the newspapers and TV were there. The publicity was good for the school, and the money raised through ticket sales was going to provide over five hundred dollars for new library books. She must have said "thank you" a hundred times.

Promptly at 8:30, the whole school assembled in the front of the school to see the inflating of the balloons. The gondolas were laying on their sides, and the balloons were stretched on the ground in the direction away from the school. A thick rope had been staked into the ground and attached to the basket. Another rope was attached to the top of the balloon and anchored to the ground. Seeing those ropes made me braver than I had been up to that moment.

Students gathered around as the burners on the gondolas started blasting hot air while balloon pilots held the envelopes (what the pilots called the balloons) open. Quickly the balloons filled, and before long, the gondolas were upright with the balloons suspended above them. I wasn't ready to jump into the basket, but the balloons were a beautiful sight.

It was nine o'clock, and the principal blew her whistle to quiet the crowd. She spoke to the guests and students, telling them how honored we were to have the balloon pilots at the school and how excited her teachers were to spend some time in the balloons "high above the ground." To that, the little voice in my head issued a correction, "thirty feet about the ground."

With her final words, it was time. The lucky teachers were ushered to the baskets where the balloon pilots gave us instructions about flying in balloons. We were assured this was going to be a safe, routine, fun ride. The plan was to rise about thirty feet in the air, remain in place for about ten minutes, and then return to the ground. A nice westerly breeze would make things brisk while we were in the air, but we were assured that the clothing we were wearing would keep us warm enough.

The process to enter the basket was very civil. A sturdy little step was placed next to the basket. Beyond that, members of the balloon's ground crew and the pilot took my hand to steady me. More than once, I heard the words, "Just relax and enjoy the ride." Ride! We were just going up a short way and then back down—that was the plan.

I mustered all my courage and moved up the step and into the basket. My students cheered and shouted to me as my feet touched down on the floor of the basket. I turned toward the crowd and could see the TV reporters chattering into their microphones as cameras were pointed at our balloons. We were still on the ground, so it wasn't too difficult to turn around and wave to them. I even managed to paste a smile on for those taking pictures. Not one of those pictures made it into the paper.

The pilot, whose name was Simon, alerted me that it was time to ascend. My hands gripped the side of the basket, and the smile fell off as hot gases shot out of the burner with a monstrous roar. More hot air was pushed into the balloon, and we started up.

The balloon's ascent was even, and to my surprise, it was very smooth. The slight breeze that I felt on the ground was much stronger once we were airborne, and I was forced to put the ball cap on. With or without the ball cap, my hair was going to be a mess, and I didn't like the wind whipping my hair over my eyes. We had gone as far as Simon planned and came to a gentle stop. This wasn't so bad at all. The burner was no longer belching flames and making a racket, so we just hung there above the school ground as the children waved and cheered. Yes, this was much nicer than I thought it would be. I managed a wave to my children on the ground. I even replied to a shout that had come from one of the other balloons. It was that crazy gym teacher rocking his balloon's basket and was doing something that looked like a high school cheer. I wasn't going to get that wild. Nope, I was looking forward to standing once again on solid ground.

Something very unexpected happened just then. There was a snapping sound, and the balloon lunged upward and to the southwest. You might wonder how I knew it was southwest. Well, that's easy. The school building was suddenly below me, and I could make out my classroom, which was on the southeast side of the building. There was no question about it, we were going southwest.

The look on Simon's face told me this trip was not going as planned. When I looked down, I could see that we were moving further and further away from the school. The open field that was below us only a minute ago was replaced with trees and houses.

Simon looked at me with a face that said, "I am in control" and "This wasn't supposed to happen." The tether that secured us to the ground came loose. We were free, floating away. The pilot couldn't land the balloon where we were, so he just continued to do pilot things while searching for a new place to put the balloon down. As for me, I can't remember much about those first few moments except I knew we were more than thirty feet above the ground. People on the ground were now shouting like that was going to bring the balloon back. Surprisingly, you don't hear things up in the sky very well, but I could make out the laughter of the children as I sailed away.

Have you ever thought about flying? I don't mean flying in an airplane or helicopter. Airplanes are noisy. I don't even mean like a bumblebee or hummingbird. Their wings make a lot of noise. I mean flying like seeds from of a dandelion, like a feather pushed along by a spring breeze, or even like a bird soaring on thermals high above a desert floor. That is what it was like in the balloon that day. We just moved along magically, suspended above the ground. Eventually, the only noise was the slight sound of the breeze that was pushing us along and messing up my hair.

Simon did his best to keep me calm, insisting that everything was fine and that there was a good landing spot about five miles away in a large public park. We could make it there in about ten minutes at the rate we were traveling. As strange as it sounds, I was as calm as if I were sitting in a lawn chair at the beach.

Suddenly, I was all in. This was turning into a most wonderful morning. I could see all over our little town; in fact, I could see across the river into Louisville. From the ground, I sometimes forgot that the river was even there, but there was no mistaking the brackish water of the Ohio River as we floated on.

The silence was lost to well-wishers on the ground. People were waving from cars, parking lots, and yards as we floated across the town. I was so enjoying the flight that I began laughing and waving back. It seemed silly now that I had been afraid of being in the balloon.

A line of cars was now following the balloon. They were honking their horns and flashing their lights as if we didn't know they were there. The van from the TV station was easy to pick out with the station's logo splashed over the side and top of the van. I once wondered why they printed stuff on the top of those vans. For some reason, it made sense now. There was a police car and fire truck in the line along with other cars that I was sure had come from the school. As a bonus to my balloon ride, I had become the grand marshal of a parade. I just could not stop laughing as we floated along.

My cell phone started vibrating in my pocket. I'd forgotten that I even had it. What a surprise. It was the reporter in the TV van below us. You would think she was reporting on the Kentucky Derby. She was shouting into the phone, peppering me with questions much faster than I could answer. I assured her that we were fine but managed to drop the phone onto the floor of the basket—the call ended.

I picked the phone up, and it immediately rang again; it was the principal. She was crying and apologizing for letting me get into the balloon. If I didn't know better, I would have thought that something bad was going to happen. Simon and I said we were fine, but she just kept going on about the balloon getting loose and something about not having a substitute for us.

We floated along for about five more minutes when we crossed over into the park, and Simon announced that we were going to land. There might have been a small hint of a frown when I first entered the balloon's gondola, but I am certain that disappointment was registered all over my face when Simon told me that we were ready to go down.

Members of his team had arrived in the park ahead of us and were prepared to capture the balloon. Simon tugged on a line that released some air from the balloon, and we began to gently return to the ground. There was some shouting from men on the ground and then tugging. I felt a slight thump, and the basket was resting on the ground.

The ride was over. I was offered a hand by someone outside of the basket as if they thought I would be anxious to be out of the gondola. I wasn't. I turned and hugged Simon. Some could have thought that I was saying, "Thank you for getting me safely on the ground." That wasn't it at all. I whispered into his ear, "Thank you so much for letting me ride with you today. Let's do it again sometime." Simon pulled away and just smiled. He knew something that I didn't know before that rope broke. The experience of flying in a balloon is indescribable. Do it once, and you will want to do it again and again.

The landing site was humming with excitement. Policemen and firefighters were trying to keep a crowd that was forming back from the landing site. There was even an ambulance there, which I did not find encouraging at all. People were streaming from the cars that had been following us, and more people were coming all the time. It seemed like a lot of fuss over nothing.

Reporters crowded, rushed toward me as my feet reached for the ground. In front of them was my dear friend, the principal. She hugged me with tears in her eyes and apologized for getting me into this mess. Several times she promised to make it up to me. How she made it up to me is yet another story. But for the moment, I just smiled and told her I was fine.

The reporters took pictures and quotes from both Simon and me. I believe that they were a little disappointed that I wasn't shaken or maybe bruised from the little mishap. With what they learned from us, they managed to have fun with our story. It was on the front page of the paper the very next day. I have a copy of that paper. The headline read, "Full of Hot Air Local Teacher Takes Off." I wanted to correct their grammar since the teacher was not full of hot air, but the article was well written and accurate, so I said nothing.

Years have passed since my balloon ride, but I can honestly say that I never see a child holding a helium balloon on a string that I don't think about my ride with Simon. I've not had the opportunity to take another balloon ride, but I guarantee you that when it does happen, I will be standing tall at the side of the basket, whooping and laughing as we float over the landscape. This time, I will be sure to take a camera and a scarf rather than a ball cap.

* * * * *

Out the Book and Into the Street

Sara was afraid of ballooning before she knew what it was like. She determined that she would not like it, without trying it or even talking with someone who had. Is there something that you are afraid to do without knowing all the facts? Is there someone who can help you understand more about the thing you are afraid to do?

FRANCIS, BOXING WITH THE BLIND

A story keeper's biggest challenge is deciding what story should be kept. In a family the size of ours, there are so many that it is impossible to keep them all. There are obvious stories. These are stories that shine with the values and character of the family—they explain who we are. Of course, there are some stories that the story keeper cannot help but keep because they are just fun, fun to tell and fun to hear.

There is a kind of story that always has a place in my library. It is revealed when I get to probing into the lives of family members. Occasionally when I am sitting with someone from the family, I ask the story keeper's favorite question. The question is, "If I can only keep one story to remember you, what would that story be?" Most of the time, the person will sit back in their chair, maybe scratch their head, and ponder the answer. Too often they just laugh and say that they don't think there is an interesting or important story about them. After some coaxing, I pull out something that causes a giant grin or maybe even a tear, but it takes some work.

My cousin Francis Angelo Marino, my uncle Angelo's oldest son, had a most surprising response when I asked him about his one, all-important story. Almost before I finished asking the question, he began to tell me his story. He didn't have to search for words or facts. It was as if Digger simply flipped a switch, the lights turned down low, and the story began to play. He narrated his story so vividly that it is projected 3D, full color, with stereophonic sound in my mind.

I must apologize. I used the name "Digger." Let me explain. Francis Angelo was his given name, but everyone, except his mother, called him Digger. I never remember Aunt Marcia calling him anything other than Francis. We heard Francis Angelo when he had done something that didn't set well with Aunt Marcia, but that is a different story. As for the name Digger, someone must know where Digger came from. I'm sure I never did.

Digger was five years older than me and my protector. I was the oldest in my family, so I didn't have a big brother; Digger accepted that responsibility as his. By the time I was ten years old, Digger was winning Golden Gloves competitions. He loved boxing. Anyone who had any sense and was not wanting to have it knocked out of him knew better than to challenge him. It's no surprise then that Digger was my hero growing up. If that was the only reason to tell this story, it would be enough. I am anxious for you to hear the story that Digger thought was the one story that should be passed on. These are his words as I remember them.

Rafa, you can't remember when I was young. I was different. I grew slower than other boys my age. I was the smallest boy in my class. Like most little guys, I was timid, and timid little guys get picked on.

* * * * *

Remember, I don't like to break in on the storyteller, but you should know something about the guy speaking. Digger past his fiftieth birthday a couple of years back. You would never know that the man telling this story was ever the little guy he was describing. Even in his fifties, Digger displayed a broad chest that rippled with muscle and arms that looked to have been sculptured from the shoulder to the wrist. Timidity, gone. He appeared as confident as any man dared to be.

* * * * *

He went on, "There were subtle things like being chosen last for games. Sometimes I was only picked because the others were not allowed to leave me out—they would have if they could. Thinking back, I realized this hurt more than being pushed around, and there was some pushing around. The main source of the shoving was a boy named Derrick."

This story is forty years old, and still I remember every taunt I received, and it seemed that Derrick played a big part.

Derrick was not really all that big, probably average for that age. I caught up with him later, but those early years were tough. Derrick was the acknowledged leader of a pack of boys from my class. You know, looking back, it is funny that he was the gang leader. When you put the bunch together, they all looked the same. He wasn't bigger, stronger, or smarter. Still, the other boys followed his lead. Because I was the smallest, I managed to get all his attention. We never fought, that was below Derrick. He didn't consider me worth fighting. There were just taunts, pushing, and every so often throwing my book bag over the fence. Derrick was a mean boy. Growing up was tough.

Rafa, you remember the house on Chestnut Drive where you came to visit? Well directly across the street from our house lived an old man who had come from the Philippine Islands. His name was Felix. He moved into that little house the year that I was in fourth grade. An older couple lived there before Felix. They didn't like us going into their yard, and so we learned to stay clear of that place. We continued to treat the house as off-limits after Felix moved in. I walked past the house, keeping my head down to avoid being yelled at just as I had with the former owners. Felix never yelled at me.

Since he didn't have any kids, there was no reason to talk with him. He did have a daughter, but she was almost as old as my mom, so that didn't count. Besides the two of them, there was a large white German shepherd at the house. The dog was far from being a puppy and was always at Felix's side. That dog never wandered out to the fence to say hello, never even wagged his tail. All in all, the family did not seem hospitable. Mostly I just saw Felix sitting in his lawn chair in the front yard, not doing anything, just sitting there. Now I know that none of this sounds very interesting but just keep listening.

I was passing in front of Felix's house after a particularly hard day at school. I don't think I was crying. I'm sure I was grumbling about a day when I would teach Derrick a lesson he would never forget. I had taken one more dose of bullying, and I was feeling sorry for myself. I was in no mood to talk. At the same time, I wanted to talk. Felix was sitting in his chair in the front yard with his head cocked to one side wearing a silly little smile. How could anyone be smiling right then? I had to climb over the fence to get my book bag once again thanks to that bully Derrick. I was dirty, my backpack was dirtier.

I just couldn't help myself, and I shouted out, "What are you smiling about?" My words were sharp. Not the words that a ten-year-old boy uses to an adult. If my momma had heard me talk like that, there would have been, well, let's just say I would have been felt her disapproval. Our conversation went something like…

"Excuse me. What did you say?" I was startled by the old man.

"I guess I was wondering what you were smiling about." No doubt about it, if my mother had heard the tone I used that day, she'd have smacked me good. My father would have done even worse. Felix just continued with his head still cocked to one side—I think he was enjoying the warm sun on his face—and smiled. This conversation started a friendship that lasted until Felix passed away.

I can still remember how the tightness in my jaw just disappears and part of a smile tried to make its way onto my face. Now, before I say another word, I need to tell you about Felix.

On the afternoon of our first meeting, Felix was in his late sixties but strong as a bull. He owned a concession that sold peanuts at local sporting events. I would see Felix carry huge burlap bags weighing more than one hundred pounds filled with raw peanuts from his truck into the house. He might stagger a little from time to time, but a younger man would have had difficulty moving those bags. Then there were those days when Felix carried the roasted peanuts from his house to the truck in those same burlap bags. He would sweat under the load, but I never heard him complain. It's hard, even now, to believe that the little old man could carry those sacks.

I'm not being unkind when I call Felix a little old man. I have already told you that he was closer to seventy than sixty. Years had stolen some of his height, but he told me he was never very tall. When I knew him, he measured less than five feet from the ground to the top of his head.

Felix's face was brown from the sun and his island birth. It showed a vast array of lines and wrinkles that he explained were a road map for all the places he had been. His hands were rough from hard work, and those hands were connected to arms that were stronger than those of most men half his age. Overall, he appeared trim, but not without signs of a few good meals. Much of this was missed by people who encountered Felix. It was his kind smile and blank stare that most people noticed at first glance. The source of the smile was uncertain, but the stare was obvious. Felix was blind. Now before you ask about a blind man's truck that I spoke about a couple minutes ago, I'll tell you that Felix's daughter did all the driving. I mean, it would have made as much sense for Felix's dog to drive the truck since Felix couldn't see.

Over time I learned Felix's story. I learned about his life growing up in Manilla, his learning to box, and people that he had met—some famous. How he lost his sight was a story that he told with the same gentle words that he used when telling me about getting his dog. It isn't very important, but I forgot to tell you that Casey was a Seeing Eye dog.

Felix grew up in the city of Manilla in the Philippines. He was the middle child of seven. Felix never said so, but I think his family was poor. His father taught him to fight when he was very young, not to be a boxer but so he could protect himself. It turned out that he was much more than a street fighter. He started boxing with a group of young men and boys at a local gym where he learned the real art of boxing. His boxing skills were better than good, and before long, he was a lightweight boxer competing in professional matches.

It was boxing that brought Felix to the United States. He fought in California, Saint Louis, Chicago, and several other cities. He even fought in Madison Square Garden once. His last fight was in Atlanta. That is where he became blind. During his last match, the laces on his opponent's gloves came loose as they were fighting. The opponent threw a hard punch that Felix avoided, but his opponent's laces whipped across his eyes. Felix reeled back from the pain of the laces only to receive a powerful right hand to the side of his head. The doctors never knew if it was the laces or the punch that caused the blindness. Felix said that it didn't matter what the cause was, either way, he couldn't see.

TALES OF THE STORY KEEPER

As I tell more of Felix's story, you will understand that I never believed that he was blind. His other senses were his vision. Felix could hear when I came into the room, and he knew his daughter was present by the scent of her bath soap. He could tell us apart, probably because I was just a stinky boy and not a nice-smelling lady. Felix had the amazing ability to tell you what coin he was given by the sound that it made when it was placed on the counter. Paper money was a problem for which Felix applied a simple rule that eliminated any confusion. He simply said that "every bill he was handed was a one-dollar bill." Some people did not like it, but it worked.

So anyway, there I was making my way home from school, dirty from having to climb down the hill to get my book bag and fuming at Derrick. I was also wondering how this old fellow could be smiling given my current situation. "What am I smiling about?" was Felix's response.

I don't like it much when people answer a question with a question. To me, it was a bad habit of old people. My parents did it all the time. My teacher would do it too. I could make a long list of old people who thought my question deserved one from them. Anyway, I replied to Felix with a simple one-word answer—that was more than he had done for me—"Yes."

You know, Rafa, I am not sure that I wanted an answer. That didn't make any difference to Felix. He was going to give me his list. He started with the weather and ended up with the price of raw peanuts. Somewhere in the middle, he mentioned his truck and the dog. It was a lot more than I needed to know. I wanted to say thank you and go on my way, but there was something about Felix that made me stay. Maybe he thought that I was older or someone else, after all, he was blind. Still, I needed to get home, so I politely thanked him and went on my way.

Over the next couple of weeks, I continued to be picked on by Derrick and have conversations with Felix. I don't guess any of that needs to be told here. Anyway, it was maybe three weeks after our first meeting that Felix asked me to come with him to see his basement. Felix, Casey, and I made our way around to a side door that opened into a den that was his basement and a lot more.

Without the aid of lights, that room would have been almost pitch-dark. Of course, Felix would not have cared. He felt for the light switch, and with a quick flick, the place was suddenly very bright. The walls were covered with knotty pine panels, and the floors were bright white tiles. The room had been converted into a small museum that contained Felix's trophies and awards. One wall was covered with newspaper clippings and posters from his fights. I would have never imagined that the boy in the pictures was the same man standing next to me in that room. I was in complete awe. Felix told me some stories, but I never imagined that my new friend was a famous boxer.

Rafa, this is the moment that changed my whole life. Yes, Felix changed everything that day.

I was standing there gawking at the pictures and trophies when Felix proposed that I should learn how to box and that he would teach me just as his father had taught him. A thought flashed through my mind where I would end the bullying and fling someone else's book bag over the fence. I didn't dare make that statement out loud. More importantly, I had no idea what learning to box meant, but I was all in.

Can you imagine being taught to box by a blind man? It is stranger than you might think. That sightless man's mind was sharp as a knife. He started with the most basic skills, moving to the next skills when he was sure that I had learned the previous. I worked the same speed bag and body bag that he had used when he was boxing. The funniest thing was when we would spar. Remember, I was ten and sighted, he was nearing seventy and blind. He didn't wear gloves, rather he had these pads that he would put on his hands. Our sparring began with me working to strike the pads on his hand as he called out commands to me. Eventually, he would smack back at me. He never really hurt me, but he popped me more than once with those pads. Remember that I said earlier that he might not be blind? When I asked how he managed to smack me, Felix would just say that he heard me or felt me. Felix claimed to be blind, but I somehow think that he must have been able to see shadows. One time I remember backing up to the wall—we didn't have a ring in his basement—trying to hide from Felix's slaps. He stood there for a couple of seconds and then turned right at me. I suppose he could have smelled me.

A few months later, the local boys' club posted a notice that boxing season was opening. Felix said that it was time for me to leave the basement and meet a sighted opponent. It turns out that the boys' club boxing was not very organized. There was only one coach who knew what he was doing, and there were lots of boys. Still, it was worth a try.

The boys' club gym was open three days a week for boys to practice. I spent most of my time in Felix's basement, so I am sure that the other boys didn't think I was very serious about boxing.

The boys' club planned match days every Saturday. After being placed into groups by size and age, we had scheduled matches. The *fight card* allowed for two matches each Saturday for each boxer.

The truth is that I was okay. Felix taught me boxing skills, and maybe he gave me some confidence, but I still didn't like getting hit very much. Also, I had received too many head-nuggies to make waves with some of the other boys. Two things happened that changed things.

Felix was the first. I remember him saying to me that we were boxing with eight-ounce gloves and padded helmets. Ten-year-old boys were not really going to hurt one another with those gloves, and even if we did get hit, the helmets would protect us. He insisted that I box just like I practiced. He said, "If you can go three rounds with a professional boxer, you can surely go three rounds with a boy." I had a hard time arguing with that.

The second thing was the fourth week of boxing matches. My first match was against a boy that I had fought a couple of times. We were evenly matched, and there was nothing ever going to be in the paper about those matches, just two ten-year-old boys with big gloves sparring for three rounds. The second match was different.

I stepped into our little ring, and there standing across from me was Derrick. The bully who had terrorized me at school was standing sixteen feet away. He was smiling that same stupid smile. When we moved to the center of the ring, he just laughed at me. The bell for the first round sounded, and we both moved to the center of the ring. I used Felix's lessons as best I could. Derrick jabbed, I blocked. This happened all through the first round. I didn't land a single blow. The second round was pretty much the same until about thirty seconds from the end. Derrick landed a right hand directly on my forehead. My head snapped back a little, but I noticed something, it didn't hurt. Derrick didn't hurt me. We finished the second round, and I am sure that Derrick was ahead in the match. I didn't care about the match; I just knew that Derrick's best punch didn't hurt.

Something changed. I was going to give Derrick all that I had. Felix had taught me well. I avoided Derrick and landed several jabs. I scored when I landed a couple of good shots to Derrick's body, and then it happened. Derrick lost his temper and was careless. He threw a wild punch and left himself unprotected. I hit him three times, the last time was a solid right hand to his head. It was so hard that I turned his helmet sideways. The match was stopped while Derrick stood there looking out of a hole that was normally where his ear was. To this day, I chuckle thinking about poor Derrick standing there in a daze, wondering why he could only see out of one eye. Of course, the other eye was covered by his helmet twisted around on his head. His headgear was fixed, and the match resumed, but there was no fight left in Derrick. It was over, and I had won.

Rafa, that was the day that I became a boxer. It was also the day that I refused to be bullied ever again. So, you see, it is easy for me to find the one story that I would want you to have. Felix remained my friend until I went off to college. I stayed in touch with him until his death. I always gave him credit for my success as a boxer and for other skills that have helped shape my entire life. Yes, Felix's lessons and that boxing match changed everything.

*****

Out the Book and Into the Street

Boxing and bullies. It might not make sense for everyone to learn to box. It might be a good idea to look for people like Felix, people that we see every day and have not taken time to speak with. You just never know what you might learn.

What about bullies? When they are resisted, they leave. We must protect the smaller, weaker around us. We must unite, friend with friend, to say no to bullying.

SOLOMON, FACE-TO-FACE WITH A LION

This story is from Solomon, my uncle on my mother's side. I don't talk about him much, mostly because I don't know that much about him. Uncle Solomon lived his whole life in East Tennessee's Smokey Mountains. I visited him a few times when I was a boy. He had a small farm, an old truck that looked to be as old as he was, and a donkey that was still older. He lived a solitary life. He never married, and as far as I know, he was content to keep a very small circle of friends. I believe this was because he liked the animals and his privacy more than people. Uncle Solomon was always kind and never shy when it came to talking about his mountain.

This story was told to me one evening when I was about ten years old. I was spending a few days with Uncle Solomon during the summer. The story is told by Uncle Solomon, but it's impossible to hide the little boy in the story.

* * * * *

It was getting late. If I had been at home, I would have been freshly bathed and sitting in front of the TV before being rushed off to bed, but not this night. There was no TV and only one small clock in Uncle Solomon's living room. The truth was that we didn't need a clock. His rooster would wake me up every morning, and I believe that Uncle Solomon woke the rooster up. He ate when he was hungry and slept when he got tired. On evenings like this one, he would sit on his front porch and enjoy the evening air. When the felt he had used up his part of the day, he went to bed. Sitting on the porch with Uncle Solomon was the best part of my day. He was so full of stories—stories about growing up in the mountains and forming "his small patch of *paradise*."

Uncle Solomon's farm was as strange a place to me as would have been the moon or maybe Mars. I was born and grew up in the city. My life was filled with street vendors, noisy traffic, and people—arm-to-arm, front-to-back people. Uncle Solomon's farm was about as far from people as I had ever been. There were no other houses or farms to be seen from his front porch. The mountain rose up behind his farm so that the sun was gone from his porch long before it set on most of those living in the area. The porch faced the east and the open fields belonging to Uncle Solomon and his friends on the next farm. This the alarm clock for Uncle Solomon and that rooster since the first rays of the morning sun fell directly onto his little farmhouse. Civilization was at the end of a heavily trodden, narrow dirt road, which led from Uncle Solomon's front porch to the paved road that went into Elizabethton. His dirt road was as old as the farm. He told me once that when he first came to the farm that he only had a Peterson wagon and a mule, no truck. The wagon was more like a big cart that only had two wheels, a large bed to carry stuff, and a small platform to sit on. I guess that old truck was a big upgrade from the wagon.

Uncle Solomon was an honest to goodness, real country farmer, living what seemed to be a hermit's existence. But he wasn't a hermit. We made a couple of trips into town, and lots of people knew him. People spoke kindly to him, and he was quick to respond with a polite "Hello." He displayed better manners than I normally saw from people at home. He always held the door open for a lady or removed his hat when he went inside. His language was sprinkled with "yes, sir," and "no, ma'am," "please," and "thank you" were also there in abundance.

So, back to the porch. When I came outside, Uncle Solomon was sitting in a well-worn cane chair on the front porch. The chair was more like a mountain throne. Uncle Solomon sat there in his bib overalls and work boots, with his ball cap covering what was left of his gray hair. His right arm was propped on the arm of the chair, with his left hand laying in his lap. He had washed up after having spent the day in the field, so his hair was clean and brushed, and not one hint of dirt was to be seen under his nails. King Solomon was holding court.

I took my place on the porch step and just waited; this was the time of day Uncle Solomon would tell me stories about his mountains. It was dark out, at least dark for a city boy. Uncle Solomon would disagree. The moon was waxing full, so we could see down the dirt drive a long way and into the nearby fields. Still, to a city boy, it was dark. The dark was joined by sounds that began to cause me fear about what was out there. The air was filled with night sounds, sounds that weren't attached to anything and unlike anything I heard at home. I know there was a low moan that could have been the growl of a bear or dragon—a boy's imagination is easily fueled by shadows and croaks from a bullfrog.

"You city people don't like silence, do you?" Solomon had finally spoken. "And you don't like the dark very much from the way you're sitting there holding onto that porch rail." I didn't think it showed.

My uncle leaned forward and pointed back behind the house. "There are things up there that could hurt you: bobcats, coyotes, foxes, wild boar, copperhead snakes, and black bears. They could hurt you, but most likely they would just go about their business." Then he sat back in his chair, silent. He sat real still and squinted his left eye a little, enough that the white completely disappeared. It was almost as if he forgot that I was there as he worked through something in his mind. He was assembling the story for the evening.

"Let me show you something." The story was about to begin.

"Give a listen out there. That's not silence, it's the night creatures having their say. It wasn't safe for most of them to wander out in the day, so they stayed home and slept. Now when it's dark, the things that would harm them have gone to their own homes, and it's safe for them to come out. Not as safe as they would like, but safer than trying to strike out during the day. Do you understand?"

I gave him a nod and a weak, "Yes, sir," but he could tell that I didn't get it.

"Do you hear those chirping crickets? They would have been bird food if they had made all that racket this morning. Do you get it?" I was trying.

"If you wander out into that field, you will find mice and a couple of rabbits running around. A hawk would have gotten them if they had been that careless this morning." I was starting to understand. He failed to mention the owls that were scanning the field that night for the same mice and rabbits.

"But there are animals out there that at night that are dangerous, right?" I was sure this was true, which logically turned some of my fear into reasonable caution.

"Yep, I already told you that there are bobcats and bears out there. But you need to understand. They didn't leave home this evening with a plan to hurt you. They are hunting for their dinner, but not even the bear has a boy-sized appetite—he prefers fish and berries to a boy. Tell me, boy, what's the scariest thing up there on the mountain?"

In a New York minute, I had that answer. I had read stories and seen pictures of cougars, a cat that weighs two hundred pounds and could run fifty miles per hour. The stories said they were "ambush hunters" that could knock down a deer with a single swipe of its huge claws. Somewhere out in the night, a cougar was hiding behind a tree or big rock waiting for me to walk down the wrong path. "The cougar!" I was sure that Uncle Solomon could not argue with my fear of cougars.

"Ah, the cougar. Well, no matter what you call them, cougar, puma, mountain lion, that animal can be a nasty fellow to tangle with, but I don't know one person to ever be bothered by a mountain lion. I've lived here all my life, and only once have I seen a mountain lion up close. I have heard them scream a few times, but then, I've heard a lot of things out there." Somehow his story wasn't making me feel any better about the dark or mountain lions. And it had occurred to me that Uncle Solomon jumped over any conversation about the bears.

"You and I need to take a walk up onto that mountain one night before you leave. It'll be a lot easier with this full moon for you to rid yourself of some of that fear." Uncle Solomon was trying to help, but I wasn't sure it was working.

"But let's talk about mountain lions." Uncle Solomon was going somewhere with his story. I'm sure that he was hoping to make me feel better, but the only way I was going to feel better about mountain lions was to know they did not live anywhere near his farm.

"Several years ago, I met a mountain lion on that path right over there." Uncle Solomon pointed to a wide dirt path that ran along the edge of his field. I never explored that path, and I immediately crossed it off my list of places to go.

"That path goes over to the Beattie farm about a mile away. You haven't met them. They are a Scottish family that has lived there for as long as I've been here. Anyway, I'd been over to dinner at their place and stayed too long. Ernie and I sat out on the porch telling stories so long that Patty came and told us good night. I took that as my invitation to leave."

"It wasn't a night like tonight. No, it was a late fall night with only a sliver of a new moon. I was carrying my trusty little flashlight just in case, but normally, I would have been able to find my way with just the light of that skinny moon and the stars. It was the fog that made things tough that night. This area has fog that sometimes settles on it. It can make night travel difficult, and this was one of those nights. So, there I was on a very dark, foggy night walking back here to the cabin." Uncle Solomon was going somewhere with this story, but up to this point, it sounded like a good Halloween story and was not helping me with the night sounds. If he had given me a sudden, "Boo," I would have leaped, no doubt with a little scream, into the yard.

Uncle Solomon continued his story. "Less than halfway home, I stepped in a hole and twisted my ankle. It hurt like the dickens. I tried to keep walking, but it was no use. I had to see about my foot. I sat down and pulled my boot off, hoping that I could rub some of the hurt out. Maybe with a few minutes to recover, I could get back on my way to the house.

"Alone, I sat there in the dark and the fog waiting for the pain to ease so I could make it the rest of the way. I wasn't afraid, just a little banged up from that hole.

"I was putting my boot back on when I heard something in the fog. There are lots of things that wander in the night, mostly raccoons and deer, but you never can be sure. I rose to my feet—feeling the pain of that bad ankle—and focused hard in the direction of the noise to see what it was. There, coming out of the fog was a mountain lion, not a cub but a full-grown mountain lion. Male or female, I could not tell. I could see that it was moving in my direction, as unaware of me as I had been of it only a few minutes earlier.

"I stood dead still and set my full gaze upon the creature. I was pretty sure the cat was male from the size of the paws. That didn't matter right then because something about me caught his attention causing the lion to freeze in his tracks and just stare in my direction. I admit I didn't know what to do. I was clueless as to what the mountain lion was thinking, but showing fear at that moment was not the thing to do." Uncle Solomon paused for a couple of seconds to gather his thoughts and to take a sip of water from the cup next to his chair.

I blurted out, "Well what happened?" I couldn't imagine how my uncle escaped being eaten.

Apologizing for the interruption, he said, "I was getting there." It was clear that Uncle Solomon was going to tell his story his way and in his own time.

With a deep breath, Uncle Solomon continued, "The two of us stood there for the longest minute the world has ever known. It took that long for the mountain lion to capture my scent. I wasn't a bear, which could've given him a good fight, or a deer, which could've been a good dinner. I was just a stinky, old farmer.

"Now don't get me wrong, I was standing face-to-face with a giant cat, and I had no idea of what to do. Running was not an option—he was faster than me, and I had a bad foot. Fighting with him was not going to turn out well for me either. I always carried my old Buck knife. It sure wasn't going to do me much good against the lion's gigantic claws. I decided that the only thing I could do was talk to him. He wasn't going to understand, but I hoped that he would sense by my voice that I meant him no harm. Secretly, I hoped he felt the same way.

"So, I started the conversation. 'Now, Mr. Mountain Lion, you are standing right in the middle of the path that I need to take to get back to my farm. I would be grateful if you would just move over there and let me pass.' At first, my talking didn't change my situation at all, but then the strangest thing happened, that mountain lion laid right down in the middle of my path. It was the darndest thing I've ever seen. That big cat pulled those giant legs up under him and stretched out the front legs to get comfortable. At this point, the best thing was that he wasn't displaying any of his big, pointy teeth that could have put an end to our conversation right away. Thinking back, he sort o' reminded me of that sphynx statue over in Egypt.

"Now what was I supposed to do?" Uncle Solomon wasn't looking for an answer, so I just sat there wondering how he got out of that mess. After all, he was telling me the story, so he didn't get eaten.

"It occurred to me that my standing over him like I was doing might not seem very friendly, so I slowly knelt to the ground. My right ankle was getting sorer every minute, so I bent down on my right knee. I wasn't completely without a plan. If quick action was required, I hoped that I could spring up quickly, but I needed to use my good foot. The left foot was going to have to do all the hard work if I had to leap to my feet.

"Once comfortable—if you can be comfortable sitting eye to eye with a huge mountain lion on a dark, foggy night—I started talking with my new friend again. The weather seemed like a good place to start, the fog was getting thicker, and the temperature was dropping. Then I think we talked about what we had had to eat that day. I was very hopeful that this lion had eaten his fill earlier that day.

"I rambled on for about five minutes when the next strange thing happened. I was in midsentence when that mountain lion laid his head down and closed his eyes. I think he went full asleep. I guess a person could feel poorly thinking that he was so boring that he managed to put a mountain lion to sleep with his rambling. It didn't hurt my feelings at all. Sleeping lions are not eating lions.

"The lion's nap gave me time to take a closer look at him. Even in the faint moonlight, I could tell that this was an old fellow. There was an expression on his face that told me this old boy was tired—he was not just resting, he was worn-out tired. He could still be a formidable foe but seemed to me that he would rather go on his way than tussle with me.

"I continued to examine the lion when the last odd thing happened, the lion started snoring. It was a real snore. Well, there was something like a purring sound, fiercer than what a house cat would make, mixed with what was a snore. That was my invitation to leave.

"I gently rose to my feet and backed away from my sleeping friend. My ankle was getting worse, so my steps were awkward. I was sure that if the lion woke up and wanted to continue our company, I would not be able to resist him. I moved far enough into the fog that I could no longer see the form of the sleeping lion or hear his snoring. My farm was closer than going back to Ernie's place, so I set my course for home by moving off the path and further into the field. It was harder walking on that bad foot through the field, but I was sure it was safer. I walked down the furrows to the other side of the field, which put me right out over there." Uncle Solomon pointed at a gate in the fence not far from where the path that he had pointed to earlier started.

"What happened to the mountain lion?" I had to find out if there was more. It just didn't seem right for the story to end without hearing more about the mountain lion.

"Don't know," Uncle Solomon's answer was short.

"Huh? You meet a mountain lion right here on your hill, and that is it?" I hoped that the old man was holding back something, maybe even a second meeting.

"That's it. There was nothing more. I never saw the old lion again. I never went looking for him, and he never came back near the farm. But that is exactly the point of this story."

I knew that he wanted to make a point, but I still wasn't seeing it. "Well, I guess I missed something because I only heard a story about a sleepy mountain lion."

"The point is this. There are lots of things in the night that can hurt you. That does not mean that they will, or even want to. Most critters that wander the night are looking for their next meal, but a boy isn't at the top of any of their menus. If you are willing to go about your business, and not get in the way of theirs, you'll be just fine. I'm not sure that it'd be good to meet a young hungry mountain lion on a foggy night, anything can happen, but then again, why would you want to wander out in the fields on a foggy night?"

The story ended right there. The night air was still filled with a thousand sounds, most of which I did not know, and I was supposed to feel better because Uncle Solomon didn't get eaten. The truth is that I did feel a little braver, but only because I was sitting on the porch with a man who could talk a mountain lion to sleep.

I was with Uncle Solomon a whole week that summer. We never went hiking in the dark, and that was just fine with me. I sat most evenings on his porch, hearing stories about the mountains, hearing sounds from the mountain, and still not sure that it was as safe out there as Uncle Solomon thought that it was. After all, nighttime city sounds, which I was used to, were just the roar of a car engine or a blaring siren from a firetruck—neither of those was likely to eat me.

* * * * *

Out the Book and Into the Street

Things that go bump in the night. We all have heard them, and almost everyone has the same reaction—fear. The sounds are worse when we are in an unfamiliar place. It is also true that people who can identify the sound are free from the fear caused by the sound.

Try to think about what Uncle Solomon was saying. Take time to learn about your environment. Put sounds and things together. Best of all, you don't have to experience the unknown by yourself. Find an *Uncle Solomon*, and discover that through knowledge, you can manage those fears.

PIA, FACING THE ENEMY

I mentioned that stories have come from different generations. This story was passed on to me by my uncle Angelo. I know the story to be true since he was the family's story keeper before me.

The story is from my great-grandmother, Pia Marino. Great-grandmother Pia lived through two world wars, sometimes living far too close to the fighting. Her story focuses on events from World War II.

* * * * *

Pia Marino was born Pia Maria Accardi in a small village between Parma and Modena in Italy. It was late in the 1800s: no automobiles, no telephones, no airplanes. Pia was the daughter of a very popular blacksmith who was sought out by people as far away as Bologna. Stories about Pia's father include iron work he did for landmarks in Piacenza. This meant that Pia's family was considered *well off* by those in their little village. The family kept a few animals for things like milk and eggs. Of course, Pia's mother had a small garden, but that was only because she liked the feel of her hands in the soil.

Pia remembered her early years as happy. These were the years before World War I—years when life was simple. Family and community were her whole life. It is easy to see Pia's kindness in many of her stories. One of her favorite stories is about Pia's father's frustration with his chickens. Pia had gone to the trouble of naming the chickens with the names of the apostles. Her father would select one to be dinner, and Pia would cry, "Please let Saint Matthew go," or "No, don't hurt Saint John." Pia saved the chickens from many close calls. She was also known as the nurse of little bunnies and stray cats.

As she grew older, Pia's focus moved from small animals to the people around her.

Pia met Georgio Marino when she was young. Georgio's family owned a modest farm just outside of the village. Georgio would come into the village to take reading lessons from the priests when it was not harvest or planting time. Some of the lessons were about math, but mostly they were about Georgio learning to read. During those trips into town, Georgio often stopped and visited with Pia.

They grew up, and as fate would have it, they married. Pia was just sixteen years old when she married. Back then, many young women married at that age. Pia and Georgio moved onto the Marino farm after the wedding where Georgio's father gave them a plot of land as a wedding gift. That was 1896, and the world was at peace.

Pia spent her days tending to the little house which Georgio had built. It was perfect for the two of them. The cottage had two rooms, one where they did all their living, cooking, and eating, and one smaller room in which they slept and cleaned up after a long day.

In 1898, Georgio's and Pia's first child arrived. Bonfila was born on Sunday, which was good since Georgio would have been out in the field on any other day. Two years later, a second daughter, Dianora, arrived. The little cottage that had been perfect for Georgio and Pia began to get crowded, and the family demanded more of the cottage and more food from the land than either could provide. In 1903, their second child, Angelo, arrived. Georgio spent the months before his birth adding a third room onto the cottage—things had gotten too crowded. Georgio also purchased another plot of land near his little farm to make sure that his growing family would not starve. There were two more children born before 1908. For the time being, the Marino family member count was seven.

Georgio, Pia, and the children worked their farm for the next few years. The ground was not the best, but hard work produced a crop large enough to feed the family. There was even surplus that Georgio sold to people in the village.

The world grew more complex, and the Marino's village was turned upside down in 1915. The world was at war, and that war invaded their village and their farm. The fighting brought a darkness on Pia. Her smiles and laughter turned to frowns and tears. Pia remembered standing in front of their farmhouse looking out over the fields. Before the war, those fields were plowed in neat lines upon which little shiny green heads of the plants poked up into the air. The war had turned those rows into deep trenches from which steel helmets hiding men's faces would peek out. Life once came out of those fields; now they only produced death. She was sure that no one in their village had offended either side in the battle, and yet both sides were destroying their homes and fields. She feared for her children and her parents who were growing older. Unlike her childhood chickens, giving the family Apostles' names could not save them from harm.

At the same time, a second tragedy, natural, not man-made, shook the land with more violence than the cannons near Pia's village. A monstrous earthquake occurred around the town of Avezzano. Everyone who lived in the town, over thirty thousand people, died.

Avezzano was a city with a short history while the region's history went back to the Romans. That history may have been part of the city's undoing. Avezzano was built in the middle of what was once a lake. The lake was drained in the late 1800s—history reports that the draining of the lake was a project that started nine hundred years earlier. What was once lake bed became fertile farmland. Good land attracted farmers, and the farmers attracted merchants to buy their crops. Twenty-five years prior to the earthquake, the area around Avezzano was home for fish, but in 1915, a thriving city had replaced the fish. And now, an earthquake had removed the people from the land.

The war moved away from Pia's farm. Evidence of fighting was everywhere, but the cannons were silenced, and wounded soldiers returned to wherever wounded soldiers go. Peace returned, but homes and crops would not come back for a long time. At the same time, Georgio received word of the destruction of Avezzano. He had no family or friends there, but the thought of so many dying there grieved him. Then there was a thought. The land around Avezzano was fertile farmland. It cried out to be tilled and planted; it needed farmers. It would be just as easy to rebuild in Avezzano, so Georgio and Pia made plans to make a new life on the plains of Avezzano. They would move their family onto the plains which were once Lake Fucino and help build a new Avezzano.

There were no signs of war when the Marino family arrived on the plains around Avezzano, but destruction there was far worse than where they had come from. The old city walls lay in rubble. No permanent buildings existed; the old city was arranged in heaps of stone, marking where building once stood. The only fresh construction was cemeteries for those who died in the earthquake.

Georgio and Pia were not the only ones to think about starting over in Avezzano. Several small parcels of land had been marked off, claimed by those who arrived before them. Shelters had been erected. These were not real buildings, just canvas structures, tents. This did not discourage Georgio since the plain around Avezzano was large enough for all who were there, and more. Georgio and Pia easily claimed a farm plot that would support their family. They were starting afresh.

Over time, the area around Avezzano came back to life. The Marino family found a new home and new friends. Pia's father and mother moved to Avezzano where he continued working in his craft, shoeing horses and creating ornate iron work. Georgio's father refused to leave the family farm despite pleas from Georgio and Pia. Plus, there were children. Two more children were born into the Marino home, twins.

Time marched on, and the children grew up. Bonfila and Dianora married and started families of their own. Angelo became an apprentice to his grandfather, then moved to Bologna to apply his trade. The twins continued to work the farm. They too married, and like their father before them, they took parcels of the family farm as their own. Georgio and Pia grew older and expected to move into their later years in comfort and peace.

Unwanted change came again to the Marino family in 1939. World War II started and saw Italy allied with the German Army. Before long, lines of soldiers were marching through the streets of Avezzano. The sounds of playing children and ringing church bells were replaced by the rattle of tanks and the roar of trucks carrying more soldiers. And the noise of war spilled further and further into the surrounding area. The Marino farm was spared from being claimed as part of the local military camp or the storage areas planted on the plains of Avezzano for now. Georgio and Pia focused on their farm and left the war fighting to others.

The Americans and their allies moved into Italy in 1940. The fighting concentrated along both the east and west coasts of the country. With the war stalled along the coasts, Avezzano was spared for the moment. The war would eventually come, but not for another couple years. It might have never come except the Germans decided to build a prison camp, a *stalag*, in Avezzano to keep prisoners captured from the coastal battles. The camp was a short distance outside the western entrance of the city, directly opposite from the storage areas which were placed just outside the eastern wall of the city.

The war was raging, but not in Avezzano. The only hint of real fighting was the daily arrival of trucks bringing more enemy soldiers to the stalag. Seldom was there a time when Pia went into town that she did not see men being led into the gates of the stalag. She later recalled that the air around the camp was foul and except for an occasional command shouted in German there was only silence. Birds that once filled the air with sweet sounds either held their tongues or moved to kinder surroundings.

It was the stalag that brought the war to Avezzano. The first sound of gunfire came from just outside the camp. An enemy airplane was flying over Avezzano. Soldiers on the ground started shooting at the plane as it circled near the stalag. The plane wasn't harmed, but the Georgio and Pia took this a sign that fighting was moving in their direction, and they were right.

Large guns were placed around the city, and the soldiers erected bunkers outside of the stalag and near the areas where supplies were stored. The Germans' actions reinforced Pia' fears—the war was coming.

The first enemy airplane had alerted others, like one bee calling others after it has been attacked. These planes were not content to circle the stalag; they bombed the supply areas and strafed the large guns which were aimed at them. The focus of the fighting was the guns and supply areas, but the planes could not prevent some of their bullets and bombs from hitting building and homes that had nothing to do with the war. The Marino farm was untouched, but the familiar sound of the battle was once again heard by Georgio and Pia. It was just a matter of time before there would be fighting in the fields outside of their home.

It was late in 1942. Allied planes attacked the German positions around Avezzano almost every night. Klieg lights would illuminate the sky just before the arrival of the enemy aircraft, and then the sound of the antiaircraft guns would fill the air. The whir of bombs followed, and explosions shook the Marino farmhouse. The effects of the war were heard and felt even though the targets were a distance away.

Pia went out on the morning after one of the nightly raids. In the field, not far from the house, she found a man wrapped in a white silk parachute. He must have escaped from a plane damaged by the German guns the night before. He was laying very still, either dead or injured. Afraid, and unsure what to do, Pia ran to the house and told Georgio about her discovery. Georgio returned with Pia to find that the pilot was alive but badly hurt. A patch on his leather jacket identified him as British.

What were they to do? They didn't want this war that was once again invading their lives. They were angry at the pilots who would come and destroy their city, and they were angry at the Germans who made targets of their city and their farm. They wanted everyone to leave and let them return to the life they enjoyed before all this started. But as they watched the pilot, blood on his face and an obvious broken leg, Pia thought, *What if that was my son Angelo?* She could not without her help. So, quietly, they moved the wounded pilot into a shed at the back of the house. The parachute became the pilot's bed and straw was his blanket. Georgio was sure that if German soldiers found the pilot in their shed, he could deny knowing that the pilot was there. Georgio would insist, "Surely this man had managed to hide himself to avoid capture." The argument would not work for long, but it would give them time to figure out what to do.

The pilot's wounds were bandaged, and his leg was splinted. It was the stranger's luck that Georgio had seen the doctor fix a neighbor's leg when a wagon fell on him. Georgio wasn't exactly sure he had done it right, but the treatment would have to do for now.

The pilot could not stay. Eventually he would be found, and then everyone would be in trouble. Pia was sure that they needed help deciding what to do, so she went into town to seek help from the priest.

The priest was easy to find. The exhausted old priest was caring for those injured during the night raids. Pia hesitated to tell the priest about the guest in their shed, especially after he had spent so much time tending wounds that could have been caused by the very one she was harboring. Still, she needed help and did not know who else to trust. So quietly, calmly Pia told her story. Each sentence contained more emotion. To whom should she give the pilot? The easy answer was to give him to the Germans. After all, they already had a prison full of enemy soldiers. There must be room for one more. Confusion and anger grew moment by moment. She finished the story in tears with the simple question, "Cosa devo fare?"

There was a long silence as the old priest seemed unmoved by Pia's story. His eyes were fixed on the floor or maybe closed in prayer; Pia couldn't tell in the light. Then the priest offered an unexpected recommendation that surprised Pia. He suggested the pilot had been placed into Pia's care. It was her responsibility to tend to him. In the meantime, the priest would help find a way to return the pilot to his own people.

The story of the pilot's return is sketchy. Pia never shared the details of the pilot leaving their farm. The events around the pilot's escape are also lost. She only said that he was turned over to a group who were going to get him safely home. We are sure that he was British; beyond that, his name and all other details are unknown.

Returning the pilot did not end the war for Georgio and Pia. In 1943, soldiers from New Zealand and Britain captured Avezzano. German soldiers were forced to flee to the north and the captives, locked behind the gates of the stalag, were set free. It was now Germany's turn to bomb Avezzano. Sides changed, but the danger to the Marino family remained as it had been since war came to Avezzano.

The war stretched on into 1944. Spring would be coming soon; the winter thaw had started. It was too early to think about planting, and seed for the fields was going to be hard to find. Still Georgio and Pia needed the distraction, so they talked and planned for their next crop. They began to clear the fields and sharpened the tools that would make plowing easier.

Pia went into the barn one morning, as she often did, and there hiding in the corner of the barn was a German soldier. She was shocked to find yet another intruder from the war on her farm. Georgio was alerted, and he came running, still grasping the pitchfork that he had been sharpening.

The soldier was too weak to resist the tines of the fork. He wasn't going to harm anyone. His appearance showed a badly torn uniform and a missing boot. There were no visible wound, so that was not the cause for his condition. Pia was sure that he had not eaten in days, and it had been much longer since he had a bath. Gazing on the soldier slumped in the corner, Pia considered that it was a German who started the war that had disrupted her life and even threatened her family. She was sure it would be years before her world returned to the way that it was—she even feared that it would never return to the peaceful way it was before the war. It was all his fault. For Pia, sending him away or reporting him to the American soldiers who were now in the town would have been easy.

As quickly as Pia's anger came, it passed and was soon replaced by something else. The German was no longer a soldier but just a man collapsed in her barn that needed help. Pia knew that she must do something for him, no less than they had done for the pilot who was there before him.

Food and water were his most urgent need. Georgio brought water from the well while Pia went into the house to get some bread, a raw potato, and a piece of dried meat. The soldier grasped the bucket and took gulp after gulp. When he could drink no more, he poured the rest over his head. He showed more restraint as he took the bread from Pia. He ate it all, but with the appetite of a hungry man, not a ravenous wolf. Once fed, the soldier laid back and closed his eyes. He was surrendered to whatever was going to happen next.

The soldier could not remain in the barn dressed in his German uniform. In different clothes, he could pass for a farmhand. In his uniform, he was a threat to Pia's family and himself. Georgio's clothes were too small, and what about the missing boot? Pia needed to go into town and seek help from an old friend.

Pia's priest had helped her before with the British pilot. Would he be willing to help with a German soldier? She wasn't sure, but it was the best hope that she had.

Avezzano's church had been rebuilt after the earthquake. Prior to the war, it was beautiful, at least for this small city. Its tall bell tower hosted a big iron bell that could be heard all over the plains and a single stained-glass window that displayed a giant cross surrounded by roses. Now, there was damage everywhere. The bell tower was still standing with the bell safely in place; however, windows were missing, including a portion of stained glass. Daylight could be seen through breaks in the walls. Stones remained in the entrance hall from where part of the roof had collapsed. This is where Pia found the priest. He was hard at work preparing for the next mass.

Pia entered the confessional and quietly waited for the priest to come to her. She knew that he could never tell anyone what she said in the confessional; this was the perfect way to seek his help. In very low voices, they exchanged words. There were dozens of questions, and Pia could only tell him what she knew. It boiled down to there was a man in her barn that needed help.

There was more conversation after which the priest agreed to help. The plan was to put the soldier into peasant clothes and pass him off as a worker on the Marino farm until he was strong enough to travel. Then they would supply him with what he needed to make his way north where the German army was still fighting. He could find help there.

Pia waited in the church while the priest worked on the details of the plan. He scurried off, returning with clothing more likely to fit the soldier and a pair of shoes. After a blessing from the priest, Pia went on her way.

Pia returned with the clothes from the priest and with a mission to get the man strong enough to return home. It wasn't as difficult as she feared. The soldier looked as if he had grown up in Avezzano once he was bathed and put on different clothes. As he regained his strength, he told Pia that his name was Friedrich and that he had family in Germany, in the town of Lindau. Friedrich spoke of fishing on Lake Constance with his brothers and missing his mother's cooking and the family dog. He was just a young man caught up on one side of an ugly war.

Friedrich's strength returned, and two weeks later, he was ready to begin his trip back to the German lines. In the middle of the night, Georgio and Pia fixed a pack with food and sent him on his way. Pia was so conflicted. She was glad to have Friedrich out of her barn. She was also going to miss the young man.

The war finally came to an end, and all the soldiers left. It took time, but the Marino family put their farm back in order. Pia lived the rest of her life in peace in Avezzano. She was well known to the people of Avezzano for her kindness to everyone. Pia never heard from the British pilot or the German soldier ever again. She wondered what happened to them and even imagined once or twice that she had seen them in a crowd. She never knew if they were able to return to their sides of the war. She didn't know if Friedrich ever tasted his mother's strudel again. She only knew that they had come to her in need and that her family did all that they could to help. She often reminded me that some war stories have happy endings.

*****

Out the Book and Into the Street

Pia reminds us that when you take away the uniform or tattoos or pink hair, people are just people. They may be more like us than we are willing to admit. And when those people are in need, our duty is to help. This is your chance to help. It could be a bread line or a day care. It could be a local church or an inner-city youth center. Determine to make a difference today.

ISABELLA, WHALE WATCHING

Isabella is my youngest sister. She has always been a free spirit. From her earliest years, Isabella has taken up the cause of the underdog and fearlessly met life head-on. There were endless petitions to protect the rain forest during her high school years. In college, Isabella took up the cause of the oceans, developing a strong love for whales and sea turtles and a strong dislike for the little plastic soda can rings that can trap birds and turtles. If you want to get her going, just mention plastic bags.

As compassionate as Isabella is about her causes, she is hugely fun. She is daring, not afraid to try something new, even a little dangerous. Isabella went bungee jumping when she was in Washington State for her fiftieth birthday and went hang gliding the next year. We thought she was crazy. She may be a little crazy; she certainly is not afraid of taking risks.

Isabella also finds humor in almost everything, and her humor frequently generates the most charming, musical, whimsical laughter. I believe that her humor is one of the things that makes her little coffee shop and bookstore a popular hangout in downtown Annapolis. Students from the university, tourists, and locals all flock to the shop to have a very good mocha latte and laugh with Isabella over the most recent political faux pas.

The story that I want to share about Isabella certainly confirms her adventurous spirit. It may take a little work, but if you listen carefully, you can hear her giggling like a naughty child as she wrings out her hair. I will let Isabella tell this story as only Isabella can. I will warn you that Isabella will be unable to tell her story without getting up on her soap box at least once.

* * * * *

We live in very important times. More than any other time, we are the voice for our environment—the air, the ground, the water. I know I can't do everything, so I choose to advocate for the water, especially for the things that live in the oceans. I didn't pick this; it picked me. I started out as a friend of the Amazon rainforest, but I was always drawn back to the ocean. That explains my personal life.

Fighting for the ocean won't pay my bills, so I needed to find a job, but I wanted my job to be as much of a calling as my love of the ocean. I found that "job" within a modest brick building on Dock Street, in the heart of old Annapolis. I stumbled onto the opportunity to buy a little bookstore near the harbor when I was looking in the window of a tiny real estate company. There was a flyer posted about a shop holding great potential in the heart of the old city. I immediately saw myself owning that "shop holding great potential."

I can see the water of the Chesapeake Bay from the front windows of my shop. The view feeds my passion for the ocean that has always been inside me. It started out to be a bookstore. I was sure the bookstore would have greater success if it also had a coffee bar. So, I expanded the shop and added a skilled barista to dispense coffees and lattes to order. We can deliver the most outrageous requests in neat little recycled paper cups that are guaranteed to satisfy. Of course, the store is a platform to inform people about the dangers being faced by our ocean wildlife. There are posters and petitions, especially for the sea turtles that live in the bay. It is my little part in the fight for the oceans.

Life is not all work. I take time off when I can to have adventures. Over the years, I have visited more natural beauty than I can tell. I made a special trip to Acadia National Park to spend the day with the puffins. I can't explain why I am so fond of those little birds; they're just so darn cute. I traveled to Alaska to hike on Mount Denali, and I wandered through the redwoods in California. I even took a guided tour on a mule to see Angel Falls in Venezuela. My story comes from one of those adventures. You won't be surprised to know that it took place on the ocean.

I bought the bookstore just before my thirtieth birthday—that would have been back in 1996. I was exhausted as we prepared to open the shop. Getting the coffee bar set up and training my staff was most of the work. I thought coffee was just coffee. I was so wrong. You have no idea what an art making coffee is. After four months without a single day off, I opened the bookstore. A month later, everything was running smooth, and I decided that I needed to take some time off.

I wanted to get away, but not too far away. There was just not time for me to leave my just-opened shop and go off to South America or Australia. It was early fall, and the whales were still feeding in the North Atlantic. There were places from the shoreline that you could see them, so New England became my destination. It was an easy choice since I could drive there in a few hours.

It wasn't just the ocean that I was looking forward to seeing. New England is beautiful in the fall. Vibrant red and orange patches are painted on every hill as the leaves turn. The weather would surely add to the trip. I looked forward to seeing blue skies dotted with wisps of white. I remembered from my last trip into the area the large seabirds drifting in the thermals caused by the warm air rising off the sides of the sea cliffs. This was going to be the perfect trip to unwind from the stress of the past few months.

My goal was to go as far north as Bar Harbor, Maine, a drive of over seven hundred miles. Driving seven hundred miles all at once is not something that I like to do, and it didn't seem like much of a vacation, so I planned several stops along the way. I am not really a fan of big cities, so I planned to drive past Philadelphia and New York, going all the way to New Haven, Connecticut. New Haven was about halfway to Bar Harbor, and there was a quaint little bed-and-breakfast there that I wanted to visit. This first leg of the journey was the longest part of my drive and the most difficult. It should have been easier except my late start forces me through Philadelphia during the lunch hour. That resulted in my circling around New

York City just as people were getting ready to leave work. Traffic was a nightmare.

I rested the first night in New Haven, getting up too late to have breakfast. Looking back, I realized it seems a bit of a waste to stay at a bed-and-breakfast and not eat breakfast. I needed the rest more than the breakfast, so I didn't think it a big loss. I spent some time chatting with the bed-and-breakfast owner, stuck an apple in my pocket, and then wandered up the coast to Bridgeport.

Wandered is too strong a word. The drive was less than thirty miles, and it took me almost three hours. I'm sure I stopped at every shop and roadside stand along the highway. I even paused for a while at a little turnout that overlooked the beach. I sat on the hood of the car breathing in the salty sea air and watching giant waves crash onto the shore. I could almost see the incoming waves deliver new sand onto the beach and then remove the old sand as the waves returned to deep water. I love the ocean and the way that it works to care for us.

I didn't arrive in Bridgeport until later afternoon. That wasn't a problem since I planned to go only as far as New Haven and spend the night. New Haven was just another thirty miles up the road, less than an hour away. Of course, the last thirty miles had taken me half the day.

Notice that I said "planned." While I was wandering around in one of the shops in Bridgeport, I saw a poster advertising whale watching tours. I love whales. I mentioned the poster to the woman in the shop. Within just a few moments, I knew that I had found a soul mate with this woman. She loved whales too! She began telling me the most fantastic stories about recent whale sightings off the coast. Several right whales were feeding just a few miles offshore. The whale pod would begin moving south very soon, but for now, they were staying very close to the feeding grounds. Groups returning from the tours carried pictures and stories that made her want to close shop and see the whales for herself. That was all I needed to hear. I was all in. My plans were flexible, so I'd go onto New Haven, spend the night, and return the next day for one of the tours. I even booked a spot on a tour before I left town.

TALES OF THE STORY KEEPER

I originally planned to stay one night in New Haven and then continue north. Getting rooms at little boutique places, like the bed-and-breakfasts where I like to stay, is difficult during the fall. There are just so many people who want to see New England during its dazzling display of colors. Anyway, I coaxed the owner of the bed-and-breakfast in New Haven to let me stay an extra night so that I could go on the whale-watching adventure.

I arose the next morning to a breakfast fit for royalty. At home, I would have gulped down a cup of coffee, from the shop of course, and maybe eaten a scone or muffin. The innkeeper was not going to let me go off without a proper breakfast. I was offered juice, eggs, meat, and potatoes. But the most fantastic part of this buffet was a blueberry casserole. I was sure that I couldn't eat another bite when she put a small plate with the casserole in front of me.

"Just take one bite," requested my host. It was obvious that she got up very early to bake the casserole, and she had been so kind to me. I was being more than polite to agree to her request.

One bite demanded a second plate of the most amazing thing I have ever put into my mouth. It was still warm, and the blueberries had forced their flavor into every corner of the pan. After embarrassing myself by finishing that second portion, I asked my host if I might get the recipe. She insisted it was a top secret family recipe but assured me that I could have some more when I next visited. I have a star next to that bed-and-breakfast in my address book.

I drove back to Bridgeport, arriving in plenty of time to meet the crew that would take me out to see the whales. Now, as much as I love the ocean, I dislike tiny boats. I saw a whale-watching tour that advertised they used large rubber rafts to get to the whale sites. Of course, the tour groups were small. It didn't matter how badly I wanted to see the whales; I was not going to pay to strap on a life jacket and bounce across the waves in one of their *Zodiacs*—just a fancy name for a tiny rubber boat.

The boat that would take me out to sea was large, maybe sixty feet long. It had a lower and upper deck from which the passengers could look out over the water. It also had a small snack bar and a bathroom. It was very civilized. I remember meeting the crew. The man identified as the Captain was a salty old fellow. He was kind enough, but all business. The remaining crew were young people, three men and two women. They did a wonderful job of making me comfortable. I never doubted that I was in safe hands with this crew.

The tour group consisted of about fifty or so people. Most came from a cruise ship that was docked somewhere close. We were all about the same age and all excited about getting a close look at one of the biggest creatures on the planet. We were given a short safety briefing that included pointing to where the life vests were stored, an offer to buy souvenirs from inside next to the snack bar, and a gentle warning to stay out of the captain's way. This was followed by a somewhat noisy departure from the pier. The ride out to the whale's feeding area would take about an hour. We were encouraged to stay alert for things we might see on the trip out.

We'd not gone far when dolphins appeared in front of the boat. It was as if they were leading the way. They stayed with the boat for a while then tired of us. Water in the North Atlantic is cold. It could have been the deeper water was a little too chilly for their liking.

I remember hearing one of the crew yelling, "Whale!" and pointing off the portside of the boat. For those not familiar with boating terms, the portside is the left side of the boat when you are facing the front of the boat. Every member of our tour group raced to the railings of both decks to see for themselves. There, about what seemed to be a block away in city terms, was a minke whale. We were bound for a feeding area where right whales were feeding, but any whale was a good start.

There was no doubt that these were minke whales, not right whales. Calling them "right whales" really does mean that there are wrong whales, at least there were when the right whales got their name. It makes me too sad to explain how they got their name, so I will just leave that to you to find out. Today, right whales are a very specific type of whale, one of the biggest whales in the ocean. Blue whales are the largest, followed by finback whales, followed by right whales. Imagine, right whales grow to be longer than the boat that I was on and that they can weigh over seventy tons, and still there are other whales that are larger.

TALES OF THE STORY KEEPER

The minke whale is a cousin to the right whale. They are much smaller. Much smaller means that they only get to be thirty-five feet long. There was a big gap between the whales and our boat. Even then, I clearly saw the dorsal fins on the backs of the whales. For one moment, I thought that I could see the white band that ran the length of the whale's body. Cameras were clicking, and those around me were abuzz with excitement. Sighting the minke whale was a good omen; we were going to find right whales when we got to the feeding area.

A half hour later we entered the whale's feeding area. It only took a few minutes to find what we had come for—right whales.

There are rules protecting the whales. Boats must keep their distance from the whales; however, whales don't have the same rules. The captain of our little boat stopped the engines while we drifted and bobbed in the waves. The whales seemed to have no knowledge of us being there. It is more likely they had their attention fixed on the small eels they were feeding upon.

One of the mysteries of the ocean is the feeding habits of these whales. It is nothing short of genius. These giant whales feed on tiny sea animals and eels. The eels didn't seem to be more than a foot long. Can you imagine a giant whale chasing down a tiny eel or a shrimp for its breakfast? If that were the case, the world would have some very skinny whales. For this reason, the right whale developed a simple and effective way to round up a meal. The right whales come to the surface and draw a giant breath of air. Then they descend and swim in a circle around the eels. As they are swimming in a circle, they blow out the air. The air bubbles form something like a cage for the eels. It's not so much a cage. The air bubbles frighten the eels, so they gather together in the middle of the bubbles for protection. Once the eels are squeezed into a smaller space, a right whale will swim up into the circle of bubbles, with mouth wide open, and scoop up a large mouthful of the whale delicacy.

Only part of this drama can be seen from the surface, and it happens quickly. First, a large ring of air bubbles comes to the surface. Soon the head of the whale will break through the water with its mouth filled with eels. I have no appetite for eels, but the whales appeared to be enjoying themselves. Also, the whale does not launch out of the water. It only rises far enough to separate the eels from the seawater—maybe eight feet.

The clicking of camera shutters was the clue that a whale was approaching the surface, and the cheers of those on the boat marked each time a whale's face broke through the water.

Remember, the whales didn't seem to care that we were there. They just repeated the feeding process over and over. The eels must have been moving toward our boat, because the air bubble rings crept closer and closer to our boat. The whales were now feeding less than fifty yards from the boat.

I had been on the second deck until then. The whales were feeding nearer the boat, and I wanted to get a closer look at the magnificent giants. The place to do that was the lower deck. I made my way down to the first deck and found an open spot along the rail near the middle section of the boat. Within seconds of my arriving, a whale popped out of the water, maybe twenty yards away. It was so close that I could clearly see the eels hanging from the baleen in its mouth.

You really need to understand baleen before I tell you any more of my story. Most people think that there are huge teeth in the mouth of a whale. Some whales have teeth, but not right whales. Inside of the right whale's mouth are these things that look like thick broom bristles. They are how the whale eats. Under the surface, the whale opens its mouth and sucks in water and everything that is in it. In this case, it was eels. When the whale comes to the top, it closes it mouth and spits the water out through the baleen. The water comes out, but the eels that are in the water stay and of course are swallowed.

Now we get to the most interesting part of the adventure. A whale descended, and within a minute or so, a ring of bubbles rose within twenty feet of the boat. We knew that we were about to get a once-in-a-lifetime view of a right whale. I leaned over the railing just a little and held out my camera. This was going to be a picture for the wall of my bookstore. Sure enough, the whale came out of the water. It was so close that I could look it directly in the eye. In the excitement, the person behind me pressed to close, and I lost my balance. I tried to regain my balance, dropping my camera into the ocean—the picture was lost. Attempting to grab the camera, I lost my balance again, and this time, I wasn't going to get it back. I think that someone tried to catch me, but it was without effect. I fell overboard, right into the feeding area of the whales.

My plunge into the water lasted only one second, maybe two, but in my mind, it was much longer. I processed so many outcomes to my situation, and not one of them was good. I imagined landing in the open mouth of the leviathan sort of like a bug flying into your mouth when you were trying to eat. I was much bigger than the eels and would be noticed immediately. Maybe I would seem like a wonderful addition, something like the whale's version of "surf and turf." Of course, that was silly; the whale's baleen would block me from getting into its mouth. The other option was not much better. I would land on the whale's head, bounce into the water, and be slapped silly with one of its flukes or fins. Right whales pack a serious wallop.

None of that happened. The whale was already beneath the water before I splashed into its dinner table. I love whales, but I was honestly frightened. I sank several feet under the water. It was dark, and I knew it was full of eels. The eels were harmless; they were also the reason the whales were there. I bobbed to the surface and grabbed a breath. I could hear shouts coming from above me. Someone was suggesting that I get back onto the boat. That was one piece of advice that I didn't need. My wish, above all other wishes, was to be standing on the deck above me. Somewhere below, where I could not see, were whales whose meal I had interrupted. I imagine that I was something like a bug falling off the ceiling into a bowl of soup. The question was, will the whales go "ew" and move to another table or just ignore it and keep on eating? I wasn't willing to find out.

In all the excitement, a white ring came flying at me from above. The life ring had a rope attached, which I grabbed onto and held tightly. The ring that I did not want to see at that moment was the bubble ring rising from below. I kept a close watch on the water while the crew worked hard to get me back onto the boat.

It took about five hours to get me back into the boat. Really, it was less than five minutes, but when you are swimming in the soup bowl of a seventy-ton whale, time moves very slowly. I know there was a flurry of activity on the boat and that the crew worked quickly to get me back onboard. I know this because one of the other passengers gave me a copy of the video he made. He captured the whole incident, starting just before I fell overboard. The video revealed that there was nothing graceful about my fall. I started over the side, my favorite sun hat blew off, and I tumbled into the water landing unceremoniously on my backside. I laugh now when I watch the recording. I wasn't laughing while floating in the water.

A man who had been standing near me when I tumbled into the water had caught my hat. He returned it to me almost as soon as I was back on deck. I burst into laughter, and others around me joined in. The moment demanded it. I was soaked from top to bottom. I half expected to pull an eel out of my pant pocket. But all was not lost; I had my unwrinkled, dry sun hat.

I was given all the free coffee that I could drink and a warm blanket as we made our way back to Bridgeport. My hair was still wet. My clothes drying out. My camera was gone, but the rest of my valuables were safe. I dropped my purse in the jostling before the fall. It remained on deck when I fell into the water.

I took pictures with the crew once we were docked. I found out later that my photo was pinned onto their bulletin board with the caption, "Biggest Catch of the Day." I also exchanged pictures and phone numbers with some of those who helped me get out of the water. We have lost touch over the years, but I still have the pictures, and they still have a story.

The right whales of the North Atlantic have become endangered. I read that they now number less than one hundred. Whale-watching tours like the one I took years ago are no longer allowed so that the few right whales still there are protected. That means that not only did I have an adventure that will not be repeated in this generation, but I can boast of swimming with some of the largest residents of the Atlantic Ocean. We were eyeball-to-eyeball. That was some adventure.

* * * * *

TALES OF THE STORY KEEPER

Out the Book and Into the Street

If there is one thing I can say about Isabella, it is that she is passionate. She did go a little overboard with the whale watching, but Isabella found a real cause that gave her purpose and made our world better. Dozens of good causes can be found just outside your door. Abandoned animals need a voice, local children need mentors to help with their studies, trash litters our streets and highways. Find your passion. Look around your neighborhood for a way to make things better for others. Don't just think about it, do something. Start by finding the phone numbers and addresses of three organizations that are in your area which have missions that you feel strongly about. Trees, turtles, tutors, whatever it is, give it some of your time.

RAFA, MY RAFT ADVENTURE

I could go on for days with stories from the family, and believe me, there are some great stories still to be told. Jonathan walking on the rim of a volcano and Josephine going skydiving for her fortieth birthday are just two of the stories that must wait until later. But looking over the stories that I have shared, I notice I have somehow managed to leave out any story about me. I will correct that oversight now.

The catalog of Papa Rafa stories is large. After all, who do I know better than me? I am tempted to tell a story that helps you see me as brave or bright, perhaps strong or sensitive. I prefer to leave you with a story that paints a very grand picture of me. There is a moose-hunting story from my stay in Alaska that is spectacular. Just the climb up the backside of Mount Denali, and the eagle sightings would make a grand story. I could also tell about riding a dirt bike across the southwest desert. That story would have to include missile launchers and tanks. But I'm not going to do that. My family stories are supposed to tell others who we are, the character of the family line. The picture can only be accurate if I include moments of failure or bad decisions. So, let me leave you with a story of bad judgment and its consequences—consequences so bad that with the smallest change in events, the family would have had to find another story keeper.

*****

There are dates that we always remember. December 25 is Christmas. July 4 is Independence Day. I have several. I have my birthday, my wedding anniversary, and the birthdays of children. Included in my calendar of eventful days is April 25, 1968. April 25 will come and go for most people without any notice. For me, it was the day I received a sobering life lesson.

On April 25, 1968, I was a senior in high school, two months from graduation, just three days before I began the most amazing job as an equipment installer. The job wasn't so amazing for what I did; it was amazing for how much they paid me. The minimum wage back then was $1.60 per hour, and my new job paid $3 per hour. You are bound to be thinking, "Why would a company hire me, an average high school senior, and pay me that crazy salary?" The answer is complicated. I took an entrance test for the company and only missed one of one hundred questions—I think I really got that one right, but the answer key said I was wrong. Scoring 99 percent was unusual for an adult; it was amazing for a high school kid. My success on the test was awarded by a face-to-face interview with the company's office manager. My dad coached me before the interview so that I would make a good impression. In 1968, boys were wearing tie-dyed T-shirts and faded blue jeans. Boy's hair length was to the collar and getting longer every day. Young people were becoming more and more radical, not only with appearance but with political views. I appeared for the interview in my Sunday suit, polished shoes, and a fresh haircut. I used the same manners that my parents demanded at home. I appeared conservative, set apart from the rebellion of the day. I was a Boy Scout poster boy from my parents' generation. I was the boy the office manager wanted. Along with a good test score and a great interview, there was one more thing, the position was a night position. They expected me to go into local businesses after business hours to install equipment. I might need to work until midnight or later some nights. I was a night owl and knew that my parents would agree if my grades didn't drop. When all that was put together, the office manager concluded I was a bright, dependable young man who was able to use good judgment to get a job done. Yep, $3 per hour in a $1.60 world.

I didn't disappoint my employer. I worked Monday, Tuesday, and Wednesday evenings. I pulled wires, mounted control panels, and connected devices all over a local warehouse with direction from the on-site manager. Good judgment and hard work paid off; my first assignment was a total success. My next assignment wasn't supposed to start until the following Monday, and I was looking forward to catching up on a couple school assignments and having a free weekend. April 25, 1968, rewrote my plans.

Thursday, April 25, 1968, started like other school days. I dressed and had breakfast with the family. I can't remember what I ate. It's not important, but you can be sure that my mother never let us leave on an empty stomach. Two of my sisters and a brother rode to school with me that day, just like every day. They could have taken the bus, but it was cool to show up and park in the senior parking lot, even if they were with their big brother. No one would have been impressed by my car. I'm sure it was an eyesore to some, a tiny little jalopy not a cool hot rod or sports car. It was old. The paint was gray and faded, the chrome was pitted, and there was some rust on the bumper. In the right setting, it could have served as a clown car from the circus, especially when we all started piling out.

The car is a central part of this story, so I should tell you more about it. I worked the entire summer between my junior and senior year to buy that car. It was my very first car. First cars are special—even more special when you work an entire summer to pay for them. The pride I attached to that 1960 Hillman Husky rivaled the pride of any new father—it was my baby. I suspect you've never heard of a Hillman Husky. It was English made. The owner's manual said that it had three doors. I always thought that it was more like a miniature station wagon. It had two doors through which four passengers could enter, five only if absolutely necessary. The third door was on the back of the car. It allowed access to a small storage space behind the backseat and a secret compartment that held the spare tire. The door opened right to left, the full width of the car. Folding down the backseats transformed the little car into a delivery van into which my mother was able to get an entire week's groceries for our family of nine. Put the seats back up, and two people could ride comfortably back there. It was tight inside when some of my football friends would squeeze into the backseat, but no one complained since it was better than walking. It's strange, but I miss that little car to this very day.

I don't want to spend too much time talking about my car, but more information is necessary. I called my Husky "Axelrod." My Husky was powered by a four-cylinder engine that was not much bigger than today's riding lawn mower engines. The owner's manual bragged the ability to reach seventy miles per hour, but I never remember that happening. Old Axelrod had a manual four-speed transmission. I changed gears with the use of a clutch pedal found just left of the brake pedal and a short shift lever that was on the floor between the two front bucket seats. If I remember correctly, I was the only one in my group of friends who drove a car with a stick shift. That didn't keep others from wanting to drive Axelrod.

Now let me go back to April 25. Oh, wait. There is something else you need to know. My high school had two campuses. The campuses were almost ten miles apart, so buses carried students back and forth. Most students had all their classes on just one campus. I was not one of those students during the second semester of my senior year. I traveled to the north campus in the morning and then to the south campus for lunch and afternoon classes. Seniors were given the privilege of driving their cars rather than taking the bus, so each morning, I loaded my car with friends and drove to the north campus. We made it a point to stop somewhere on the way back to the south campus for lunch. We could grab a hamburger and get back to school well before our lunch hour ended. Now back to April 25.

Morning classes ended as normal. A bell rang at 11:00 ushering us out of the classroom and back to the other campus. Wait! Oh, there is one more thing you must know. There was a raft, an inflatable rubber raft.

A week or so earlier, I bought a rubber raft from Joel Alderman—actually, I traded an old arc welder that I'd found and repaired for it. I didn't know where Joel got the raft or why he wanted to trade it. I didn't care. I planned to sail into great adventures in that little raft. The trade included a pair of oars, a foot pump, and a rope tied to the bow of the raft which must have been twenty-five feet long. I got a real deal. The raft was big enough to squeeze in two people, but I planned to be a one-man crew. I envisioned myself rowing the raft up and down the river or in the lake, just me and the water. Maybe I would take it out into the bay or up into Lake Champlain. Boundless prospects awaited me.

I've already told you that morning classes were over. Joel met me at my car and transferred the raft into the back. It was all mine. Packed into the back of my car, the raft was unimpressive. It was rolled up tight with the rope keeping it from spilling out of the back compartment. It resembled a bedroll or maybe an old canvas tent more than a watercraft. Chances were you wouldn't know what it was unless you were told. The oars might be a clue, maybe not.

I loaded my friends into Axelrod, and we started for the south campus. I was driving. Linda was in the front passenger seat. Sherman and Wayne were stuffed in the backseat. Before we could get out of the parking lot, the vote was taken, and a lunch site was selected. I pointed the car in the direction of a nearby McDonald's.

The guys in the car wanted to talk about the raft. They doubted it would inflate and were pretty sure it would never float. Bets were made; I defended the raft. Linda didn't care about the dusty old raft and worked to change the subject. She began to ask questions about the car. She was intrigued by the shift lever. Linda was sure that it was hard, too hard for her to learn. That was where the day took a turn for the worse. I argued that she was wrong and that I could teach her in just a few minutes. Thinking back, I was taking bets with everyone that day. Linda could learn to drive my car and the raft would float.

We stopped listening to each other and went into full defensive mode. It was, "Yes, you can!" and "Yes, it will." I argued with all of them—three against one. We turned onto a back street that led to McDonald's when I had all that I could take from the three of them. I stopped the car and demanded that Linda get out. She probably thought that I was throwing her out, but I had other plans. I ordered her into the driver's seat and took my place where she had been only a minute earlier. Sherman and Wayne became dead silent.

I gave Linda a quick tutorial on using the clutch and the shift lever and then had her practice starting and stopping the car. Put your foot on the brake, press in the clutch pedal, move the shift lever into first gear, let out the clutch pedal while pressing lightly on the gas pedal. We repeated those steps a dozen times or so; then, we moved to the next step. Linda would shift between first and second gear. She had to go a little faster for this part, maybe twenty or twenty-five miles per hour. We made our way up and down that street several times. She did it, stopped, and she did it again. After about ten minutes, I declared myself a master driving instructor.

Linda parked the car, and we were about to exchange seats when the guys in the backseat started again about my raft. The laughter was mixed with comments about the "giant rubber jelly roll" behind the seat. They were sure it would not float. They didn't think it would inflate. Sherman was complaining that I had traded away a perfectly good arc welder for a rubber inner tube with holes in it. By the way, I don't have any idea what I would have done with that arc welder if I had kept it, so it wouldn't have been a great loss if the raft was full of holes.

I was fed up with being the center of their jokes. Linda had learned to shift gears just as I promised. Now I had to deal with the two yahoos in the backseat. Instead of going to the driver's side door, I move directly to the back of the car. I grabbed the handle, threw open the door, and pulled the raft onto the pavement. I then ordered Wayne and Sherman out of the car. They were going to help me blow up the raft.

We quickly untangled the rope and stretched out the raft on the street. Wayne expressed the greatest doubt that the raft could be inflated, so I demanded he start pumping. After a couple minutes, Wayne asked Sherman to pump for a while. We all took turns, and after a few minutes, the raft was inflated to its full length. It was dusty, even a little discolored from the sun, but it was inflated, and there were no signs of leaks. I was sure that I had gotten a good deal, maybe a better deal than Joel.

It would be great if the story ended here: Linda proved she could learn to drive a stick shift and the raft proved to be seaworthy. Unfortunately, there was more.

We stood there looking at the raft, and then one of us—I don't remember who—commented that is was a shame that we worked so hard to inflate that raft without a chance to put it in the water, and now we needed to release the air. "Release the air" stopped short of saying "without doing something sensational with the raft."

Three teenage boys, regardless of how responsible you might think they are, can come up with some dumb ideas. Given a little time, they can take a dumb idea and turn it into something most superheroes won't attempt. This was one of those times.

We decided to commission the raft with a maiden voyage. We were far from water, and there was still the second half of the school day for us to finish. We had lost time to the driving lesson, and we still hadn't eaten. Whatever we did must happen soon and be brief. The initial plan was simple and safe. Wayne and Sherman would pull me across the grass using the rope. The plan was rejected fearing that the raft would tear either from pulling or the grass.

Hmm? How do you keep the raft stationary and have it move at the same time? It came to me in almost a divine revelation. We would put the raft on top of Axelrod. The tow rope would be tied to the bumper, and the guys could put their arms out the windows to keep it steady. It seemed like a perfect plan—the raft would be in motion while sitting still. I, of course, would sit in the raft as we slowly made our way along the road toward McDonald's. My weight would help keep the raft on the roof and I would look cool sitting there like Captain Jack Sparrow.

Getting into the raft was harder than you can imagine, but I managed it. I scooted along the canvas bottom until I was as far to the rear as I dared and secured my feet along the side. Linda handed the oars to me, climbed into the driver's seat, and closed the door. It was right about then I began doubting the wisdom of our plan, but I had gone too far to turn back.

Linda was the only person in the car who knew how to operate the stick shift, so she had to drive. Then again, Linda had only gained that skill minutes before I entered the raft. She was going to go slow, probably never leave first gear, so it should be okay. We did a quick review of shifting with an emphasis on slow and smooth.

I announced that I was ready, arms from the guys in the backseat sprang into place, and Axelrod began to move. Linda was amazing. I couldn't have done better. This was going to be something to tell my children about.

We grew bolder. I moved the oars in the air fighting the current. Wayne and Sherman steadied the raft, but there was nothing for them to do. The raft was firmly seated on the roof of the car, and I was firmly seated in the raft. Our boldness translated into Linda putting a little more pressure on the gas pedal. We were going faster, fast enough that Linda decided to shift into second gear.

Everything was exactly as planned as we moved further down the street. No one remembers how fast we were going as we neared the corner by McDonald's. Everyone is clear on what happened as Linda steered through the turn.

I thought Linda was going to stop the car before we made the turn. Linda thought so too. As we neared the corner, Linda stepped on the pedal to stop. She mistakenly stepped on the clutch pedal instead of the brake pedal. The car didn't slow, and the corner was quickly approaching. She had no choice but to turn the wheel and guided the car through the turn. The raft did not receive the same guidance instructions as the car, so it stayed on its original course. Neither Wayne nor Sherman could hold on, and the raft broke loose. Axelrod went right while the raft and I continued down the road.

The next flaw in our plan was that safety rope. We tied it to the bumper. I was sitting, somewhat confused in the raft as the car turned away from me. Suddenly the rope when taunt, and the raft returned to the car without me. Sherman later told me that the raft flew back to the car, smashing into the driver's door. He could be right; however, at that moment, I had lost all concern for either the car or the raft. The raft had abandoned me to free flight, and I was losing airspeed and altitude fast. I received a short object lesson about gravity and momentum. I remember spinning around in the air, briefly traveling backward, and then landing in the street. Momentum drove me backward, and I slid on my back along the pavement, coming to rest against the curb.

I don't know how long I laid in the street, or much else after that until late afternoon. I awoke in the emergency room. It was a mystery how I got there. I later found out that the elbows of my jacket and the belt that I wore were both worn completely through by my sliding down the pavement. I also found out that Sherman had called my parents from the McDonald's and that my dad took me to the hospital. So, there I laid with a bloody bag of ice on my head and my parents staring down at me. For the time being, they were happy that I was alive. Later they expressed their disappointment.

I had time to replay and rethink the events of that day over and over. My scorecard always came out the same: thirteen stitches in my head and two missed days of school, more gray hairs for my parents from worry and hospital expenses, and three friends put into a difficult spot—one thought that she had killed me when I landed on the pavement. I couldn't count one positive thing no matter how hard I tried.

It was the biggest failure of my high school years—two extremely bad choices at the same time. I let Linda drive, and I rode on top of a moving car. The only good thing that came from that day was that I began a serious practice of thinking through things before I put them into motion. I didn't become afraid to try things. I still jumped off a bridge into the river and parachuted out of an airplane. The difference was that preparations and precautions became a part of my daring adventures. Quick responses from pride or anger were easily dismissed by simply rubbing the back of my head—the scar from the stitches can still be felt. So, you see, I tell this story as a warning to others and a reminder to me. Think before you act.

*****

Out the Book and Into the Street

Most adults have something in their past they can point to and say, "I shouldn't have done that." You may know exactly what I am talking about. Hopefully, it wasn't too painful and something was learned from it.

It's easy to find yourself about to do something that is not exactly safe. From inside, you can hear a little voice saying, "Shouldn't you think about this?" or maybe "Your mom is not going to like this."

The question is, "Are you willing to listen to that voice and give some more thought to what you are about to do?"

Something else, do you have a friend whom you can ask to help you? A friend you trust to help you make good decisions. Seek out those friends, keep them close. I have stories that I can tell that were the direct result of confiding in trusted friends. They all have much better endings.

ABOUT THE AUTHOR

Ralph Berwanger might be the guy next door. He is a husband, father, and grandfather. He likes to keep his yard cut and his car clean. He lives with his wife, youngest son, and three dogs. He plays softball, coaches' soccer, and cheers for his son's football team from the stands. There is more. He was a warrior for more than twenty years; a leader for a United Nations working group; a consultant to government, financial, and healthcare organizations; a principal within commercial and nonprofit organizations; and a mentor to the next generation of leaders. He has enjoyed three lifetimes of living and isn't done yet. Storytelling has been a tool used by Mr. Berwanger in almost every position he has held. He uses stories to teach and educate. His stories have been valuable aids for relationship building and compromise. Mr. Berwanger sees his stories as music, told with pitch, meter, and rhyme. Some stories are sacred—not one detail will be allowed to change. These have perfect fidelity to time and space. He feels free to take license with others which are spun a little this way and a little that. Mr. Berwanger is confident that the way the story is told is the way that it should have been.